1

Caldon Manor

Amid the flat and densely wooded countryside of Berkshire, England, the hill with the ruined castle perched on its summit came as quite a surprise to Elva Reeves. For half an hour the slow train had been grinding through more or less uniform landscape, splashed with the usual offerings of cows, sheep and June sunshine — and now there was this. Elva found the hill a relief in the monotony, and contemplated it with interest.

Elva shifted her gaze to her solitary traveling companion who had accompanied her from London. She was a frigid-looking woman who throughout the journey had been absorbed in a book blatantly advertising itself as concerned with the rights of women in society.

'I'm on my way to Caldon Manor,' Elva said. 'In the letter I had from there, giving me directions, it says that Theston Mount can be seen from the Manor. It's a sort of landmark, I understand.'

'Theston Mount can be seen from anywhere in Caldon village,' the woman answered. 'I ought to know. I've lived in Caldon all my life.' Pause. 'From your accent, you are a Midlander.'

'Selly Oak,' Eva said. 'That's just outside Birmingham. My name's Elva Reeves.'

The woman's glacial eyes wandered up to the girl's single big suitcase on the luggage rack, then back to the girl's face. Beauty as such, was not a quality that appealed to this torch-carrier of women's rights — but in this instance she had to admit that it was present. Elva Reeves had more than her share of looks and yet did not convey the impression that she was aware of it. There was about her a quiet simplicity, underlined by the un-decorative cotton frock she was wearing. Her hat was modish enough, but inexpensive; her coat on the seat beside her was ordinary.

'I am Agatha Dunwiddy,' the suffragist stated. 'I'm the leader of the Caldon

Woman's Movement. Miss Agatha Dunwiddy,' she emphasized, and a glitter came into her ice-blue eyes as she added: 'and I intend to remain so! There is so much a single woman can do, hewing a path toward equality.'

'Yes, indeed,' Elva agreed, in polite wonder.

'Are you a relative of the Caldons?'

'No. I'm the new parlour maid. That is, if my work is suitable. They seemed satisfied enough with me at the interview. That was in London. I've never been here before.'

'Whom do you mean by 'they'? Drake Caldon is the owner of Caldon Manor and he's unmarried.'

'I saw the butler and housekeeper.'

'Yes, of course. Mr. and Mrs. Carfax, the butler and housekeeper, are married. Been at the manor many years.'

Elva became silent, and the man-eater was again considering the unusual beauty of the girl.

Flaming red hair swept down in cascades to her shoulders, and in spite of her efforts with pins and gadgets it escaped at the side into curls and wisps, each one of which became a glittering bright copper coil in the sunlight. It was superb hair, magnificent hair. Of itself it would have redeemed any face — only the face of Elva Reeves did not require redemption.

It was a perfect oval, the cheekbones high but not obtrusively so. Instead of the colourless complexion and pale blue eyes, which frequently matches such hair there were deep violet eyes and delicately pink cheeks. The lashes and brows were black and full, the mouth firm and well shaped. In every turn of her head Elva revealed a perfection that was natural and unaided by a single cosmetic.

The leader of the Caldon Woman's Movement cleared her throat.

'You are gifted with unusually good looks Miss Reeves,' she announced, as if conferring a favour.

Elva shrugged. 'Frankly, I'm one of nature's extra good jokes, otherwise I'd be a showgirl. I know it. No sense in disguising it. I've got the looks, but unfortunately they are not everything.

The picture's incomplete, you see.'

'I don't see. There's nothing wrong with you.'

Elva only smiled. After a while she asked a question.

'I suppose you know Mr. Caldon?'

'Yes.' Long pause, and the woman looked out of the window. There was something in her expression, which, to Elva, suggested that Agatha wanted to forget something unpleasant. 'I know both of them — Drake and his brother, Arthur.'

'I didn't know there were brothers. Do they both live at the manor?'

'They did; then they quarreled and separated. There was quite a lot of gossip about it at the time. I've little doubt that you'll pick up the details before you have been very long at the manor.'

The train began to slow down, and Elva stood up — she was about five feet five — and hauled down her suitcase. And oddly, when she had the case beside her, on the seat she seemed to shrink a couple of inches and stand one-sidedly. It was not until they were off the train together that Agatha realized the reason.

Elva Reeves, for all her phenomenal beauty, had been right in saying the picture was incomplete. She had one leg somewhat shorter than the other.

With the observation that she had to go 'this way', Agatha Dunwiddy took her departure. Elva put down her suitcase and looked about her. There was no sign of a taxi.

'Can I get a cab from here for the manor?' Elva called back to the man who had taken her ticket.

'I'm afraid not, miss. There's only one and its been hired to take a party to the garden fete at Lady Clarden's.'

'How far is it to Caldon Manor?' Elva asked.

'About two miles. Keep going straight on down the road there. You can't miss it. Bit back from the road it is — big ramblin' sort of place. Teller gate posts.'

Elva picked up the suitcase and started to walk. It was unpleasantly hot and the case was heavy.

2

Incomplete Picture

She went through the village, and after walking for a mile she came to crossroads and stood wondering which fork to take. Neither of them referred specifically to Caldon Manor but to the next nearest town: Barrington one way, and Kilhampton the other. Elva set down her suitcase and bit her lip in annoyance. Then she turned at the sound of an approaching car.

A young man was at the wheel and he stopped.

'Want a lift?' he asked.

Elva did not answer immediately. She was summing him up. He was darkly handsome with black hair. His worst feature was his mouth — large, even somewhat dissolute about the lower lip, yet redeemed by perfect teeth. His brown eyes were inquiring — or perhaps even insolent. His long, straight nose gave him a sarcastic expression.

'I'm wondering which is the right road for Caldon Manor,' Elva said.

For some reason his expression changed, It changed again as she moved toward him. She had been standing in what seemed to be a relaxed pose. Now her slight lameness became noticeable.

'I'm not going past Caldon Manor,' he said. 'Sorry.'

'That surely doesn't prevent you telling me which road it's on.'

'It's the one on the right. The manor is about half a mile farther on. Yellow gateposts. Are you a friend of the Caldons?'

'You don't think a friend would be left to carry her own luggage a mile and a half at 80 in the shade, do you?' she asked coldly. 'If you must know, I'm the new parlour maid.'

'Well, best of luck!' the man said, and drove away.

When Elva arrived at the manor, the butler, Carfax, and his wife treated her exactly as she had expected to be treated, as being entitled to indulge in backstairs gossip, but not permitted to take advantage. The housekeeper, a smallish, dumpy woman, whose hair was nearly white, showed her to her room and said in a crisp, chirping kind of voice: 'Your duties will commence with dinner this evening, Reeves. If you are puzzled about anything, either ask Mr. Carfax or me. You will be expected to dine with us in the kitchen at 6. The master and Mr. Wood dine at 7.30.'

Elva put on her uniform and brushed her gleaming red hair. She put the contents of her suitcase into the dressing table drawers and wardrobes, tested the bed and wagged her head approvingly. Then she considered the view from the window. The manor had extensive grounds, a long curving driveway losing itself in the avenue of elm trees. The flowerbeds and impeccable lawns testified to the work of a master gardener.

A man, very broad shouldered though not particularly tall, dressed in sports coat and grey flannel trousers, strolled up the drive with what looked to be several ledgers under his arm. Elva watched him interestedly and noticed as he came nearer that he had curly fair hair. He glanced upward idly and then continued on his way to the front door.

Was he the 'Mr. Wood' whom Mrs. Carfax had mentioned? Elva suddenly made up her mind. She gave her hair a final touch and then left the room. In the corridor she glanced toward the service stairs, which the housekeeper had pointed out to her, but Elva went to the main staircase.

She descended it so that her limp was not noticeable as she went down stair by stair. She congratulated herself on her timing. The young man with the ledgers was just crossing the wide parquet-floored hall.

He glanced briefly in her direction, looked away, then looked back again at her. He paused.

'You're new here,' he said, with a half smile. He had a quiet, rather slow voice.

'Yes, sir. I'm Reeves, the new parlour maid.'

Elva came to the bottom of the

staircase and paused, her lame foot on the lowest step so that the defect was not noticed.

The young man's face was round and fresh-complexioned.

'I hope you'll be comfortable here, Reeves,' he said, and went on his way across the hall, vanishing beyond a carved oak door. Elva wondered if perhaps it might be the library. As yet she knew nothing of the manor's layout.

Suddenly she remembered where she was. She returned quickly up the staircase, found her way back to the east wing, and descended the service staircase and entered the big kitchen.

Carfax, the butler, was seated in his shirtsleeves reading a newspaper. His wife, the housekeeper, was apparently checking over a domestic list of some kind, while a rather thin-nosed kitchen maid was busy at an enormous sink. A chauffeur, judging from his bottle-green breeches, was wringing out a cloth into a bucket, his sleeves rolled back to his elbows.

'Cor!' he commented, and whistled

under his breath as he saw Elva approaching. His eyes followed her intently, but something of the absorption went from him as he detected the limp.

Mrs. Carfax gestured. 'This is Gerald Binns, the chauffeur-handyman. And this is Ethel, the scullery maid.' She looked at the man and the girl in turn. 'This is our new parlour maid, Elva Reeves,' she added.

'Mighty glad to know you,' the chauffeur exclaimed.

'Mr. Carfax you have already met,' Mrs. Carfax added. 'That comprises the staff, except for the char. I am also the cook. Labour shortage has hit us hard, but we manage to get along satisfactorily.'

'I'm sure you do,' Elva agreed. 'By the way, you did say I might ask any questions about the place?'

'Certainly,' the housekeeper assented.

'Well, it's only a small question,' Elva had an entirely innocent expression. 'I saw a man coming toward the manor carrying ledgers under his arm. Who might he be?'

'Barry Wood, Mr. Caldon's cousin,' the

butler answered, looking over his newspaper. 'On his mother's side, of course. In a sense he is Mr. Caldon's business manager, handling the rents and dues of the estate.'

'He looked rather nice,' Elva commented.

Carfax got to his feet. He was a very tall man, middle-aged, with neatly brushed grey hair. The extreme length of his face and nose gave him a mournful aspect. Normally his grey eyes had a completely aloof expression as though he were looking at something on another planet, but for the moment they had lost their look of distance. They were fixed steadily on Elva.

'I think, Reeves, before you commence your duties, that there is one thing you should get absolutely clear,' he said. 'It is no concern of yours whether the people outside this domestic sphere are nice or nasty. You are simply here to take their orders. You will be good enough to keep all opinions to yourself.'

He paused and his eyes wandered to Elva's hair. 'Is there not some other way of doing your hair?' he questioned.

'What's the matter with it? It looks all right to me.'

'It's conspicuous,' Carfax stated.

'You mean perfect,' the chauffeur said, grinning.

3

Identical twins

Carfax said nothing but his eyes strayed to his wife. She said nothing either — at least not immediately. When she did speak her statement was more or less ambiguous.

'It might be to your own ultimate benefit, Reeves, to make yourself less attractive.'

The butler said: 'I will outline your duties at the table, Reeves. Each household has its own particular system . . . '

When Carfax had explained how to go about serving, Elva found herself with the chauffer-handyman. He proved to be an easy-going, communicative chap and not overburdened with tact. By degrees, as she attended to various small tasks attendant on dinner being properly served, Elva wormed out of him several facts concerning the household.

There were only two men to cater for — Drake Caldon, whose time was largely taken up in business deals in London, and his cousin, Barry Wood, perambulated between the manor and the village, occupied with the affairs of the estate. Drake's brother, Arthur, left after a violent quarrel.

'Decent bloke, Mr. Arthur,' Gerald said. 'Painter, he is.'

'Painter?' Elva repeated. 'Do you mean an artist?'

'An artist. He dabbles at painting for fun. Can't be for money: bags of it in the family. He lives at a cottage not far from here. Manor property . . . '

He had no opportunity to say anything more — and neither had Elva. The time had come when she was on duty. She remembered everything that Carfax had told her and she entered the dining room with her tray. At once she was faced with a tremendous task in keeping control of her emotions.

Barry Wood, with his curly fair hair and broad shoulders, she had already seen, of course. He was seated at the perfectly laid table, smiling as though to himself. It was the other man, presumably Drake Caldon, who nearly caused Elva to drop the tray and shatter the silence of the big old-fashioned room.

It was the man she had seen at the crossroads and who had said he was not going past Caldon Manor.

Though her mind was in a whirl, Elva went through her duties perfectly. She was unobtrusive, silent, and alert for every detail. Once or twice she caught Barry Wood absently studying her — but Drake Caldon did not appear even to notice she was present.

She had plenty of opportunity to study him and it only deepened her conviction that he was the same man who had not been over-helpful. He did not show the slightest sign of recognizing her.

Anyway, why should he? But she thought that perhaps a friendly smile might have escaped him, if only to put her at her ease in a strange place.

Throughout the meal he confined his conversation to statements concerning land and rents, about which his cousin seemed to have all the answers. The voice, too, was the same, Elva noted. Brusque — matter-of-fact.

When her serving duties were over, Elva could not keep the matter to herself and told Mrs. Carfax.

'You met the master? This afternoon?' Mrs. Carfax repeated in surprise, and her husband looked round from considering the remains of the dinner.

'At the crossroads,' Elva emphasized. 'I asked him the way to the manor. He said he didn't go past it but he did tell me where it was. Didn't go past it, mind you!' she repeated. 'Next thing I know he's seated at the dinner table!'

Mrs. Carfax's surprise passed into good humour.

'You didn't see Mr. Drake Caldon, Reeves,' she said, 'because he's been in London all day. Drove himself there. The mistake was a natural one. You saw his brother, Mr. Arthur. They are twins, you know.'

The butler said: 'The only distinction between them is that Mr. Caldon parts his hair on the right side, and Mr. Arthur the left.'

'The master is the elder. By half an hour,' the housekeeper said. 'Mr. Carfax and I were present when they were born. Mrs. Caldon died before they were two hours old. The half hour made all the difference between Mr. Drake being the master of the manor instead of Mr. Arthur. There was some dispute when Mr. Caldon died eight years ago.'

'Was that when the quarrel happened?' Elva inquired.

'No. That was three years ago.' Mrs. Carfax was slowly drawing back into her formal shell. 'We never found out the real reason for it. All we know now is that Mr. Arthur has a cottage with a garage attached about half a mile from here where he pursues his hobby as an artist. Money he has in plenty. The will divided the money into equal shares, but the manor went to the master together with all the land and property.'

'I never saw two men so much alike, even to the voices,' Elva said.

'Physically,' the housekeeper said, 'they are identical.'

This definitely implied more, but Mrs. Carfax knew where to stop, and Elva knew when questioning ought to cease. Then Carfax glanced up as the bell signalled from the drawing room.

'I'll attend to it,' he said, as Elva half lowered the glass she was polishing and be went out pulling his coat sharply into position. When he came back, in perhaps five minutes, there was menace in his long, horse-like face.

He said: 'For what reason, Reeves, did you come down the main staircase after you had arrived this afternoon? I am sure Mrs. Carfax was at pains to show you the servants' stairway.'

'Yes, I — ' Elva hesitated. 'I mistook my way.'

'Indeed? Then see it doesn't occur again. The master has just been remarking — I might even say complaining — to me about it, so you must be more careful in future.'

'He couldn't have known without Mr. Wood having told him,' Elva pointed out.

'Mr. Wood did tell him,' Carfax said.

It interested Elva deeply that the incident had been considered worth mentioning. She wondered if the two men had been discussing her and the incident of the staircase had turned up.

4

The artist

For the next two days Elva only saw Drake Caldon at mealtimes and be remained as impersonal as ever, unless it was to pass a remark that this or that was out of place. He seemed to have a positive mania for having everything just so. Not so his cousin, from whom Elva received many a generous smile of thanks. She accepted the smiles for what they were, thinking no further. She had learned enough in the short time she had been in the manor to know that Barry Wood was not worth running after. What money he had was through the will in the form of a salary, as manager of the estate. Or so said the chauffeur who seemed to be an expert at ferreting for news.

Having pushed Barry Wood out of her mind as a possible man to help her climb the social ladder, it came to Elva as a decided shock to find him suddenly taking the initiative. It happened on her third day at the manor, the afternoon and evening of which she was entitled to take off.

She decided to spend the fine summer day exploring the surrounding countryside. She found a quiet lane that began at an outmost point of the manor grounds and wound its way through banks of grass, bracken and overhanging trees in a small cottage surrounded by a low wooden fence. Within seeing distance of it she stopped wondering vaguely who chose to live there. It was not a particularly old cottage and a modern brick garage was at the side of it.

'And just what is Miss Reeves wondering about now?'

Elva turned and saw Barry Wood only a few yards behind her, a ledger under his arm. Though from this he appeared to be on business bent, his grey slacks, blazer, and open-necked shirt suggested otherwise.

'Oh, Mr. Wood!' Elva gave a slow and somewhat embarrassed smile. 'Good afternoon, sir.'

'Sir?' He grinned good-humouredly and looked at her with twinkling lights in his blue eyes. 'How absurd! You're off duty now, remember.'

'Well, yes, I am, but — '

'There are no buts about it, Miss Reeves.'

It flashed through Elva's mind that perhaps he had followed her. She wondered whether she ought to feel flattered by the possibility. The pity was that, as far as she was concerned, it could not lead anywhere. It was Drake Caldon who held her interest — not as a man but because of his money and position.

'I'm rent collecting,' Barry Wood explained amiably. 'Sometimes Mr. Caldon does it, but today he's gone to Barrington.'

'I see,' Elva murmured, though she wondered if it were really necessary to traverse a lonely lane in order to collect rents.

'I'm collecting at the cottage,' Barry went on. 'Mr. Caldon's brother, you know. That's where he lives.'

Elva said: 'Oh, of course. I remember Mrs. Carfax saying something about it. I believe he's an artist.'

'Uh-huh. Only a hobby, mind you. He never did anything good enough to hang in the Academy. Or even to sell. Landscapes chiefly. Spends a lot of time around Theston Mount painting the views from there.'

'Oh, yes — that ruined castle?'

'That's right.'

Silence.

'Smoke?' Wood held out his cigarette case.

'No, sir. Thanks all the same.'

He smiled, lighted his cigarette, and motioned to the tall bank of grass. Because there seemed to be nothing else for it, Elva seated herself beside him.

'Surely a girl with your looks has no need to be just a parlour maid,' he said.

Unconsciously Elva's eyes strayed to her lame leg. Wood added:

'That doesn't signify. You have the kind of face a magazine artist would give his shirt for. Your foot wouldn't enter into it. Take Arthur Caldon, for instance. He'd go into ecstasies if he could only see you . . . Why don't you come and let me introduce you to him?'

Elva got to her feet.

'This is going to make my employment at the manor most embarrassing, Mr. Wood,' she said. 'I can see the spirit in which you're trying to forge a friendship, but I'm sure it would be better for both of us if you didn't.'

★ ★ ★

Barry found Arthur Caldon at work in the sunny back room, which he used as a studio. He was dressed in grey flannel shirt, and corduroy trousers, squatting on a stool in front of easel and canvas. A none too good painting of a bowl of flowers was taking shape there, the original being on a small table in a corner.

'Hello, Arthur!' Barry greeted.

Arthur Caldon glanced round, an exact replica of his brother except for the left-hand parting in his black hair. Only in expression was he different. The tendency to sardonic aloofness so apparent in Drake was absent here.

'Oh, it's you, Barry! Came to rake in

the rent for that grasping brother of mine, eh? Wonder he didn't come himself and make sure.'

'Matter of fact, he's in Barrington on business. Went on a bus for a change, too. Sorry I have to collect, but its orders.'

'I know,' Arthur Caldon said, shrugging. He put down his paintbrush and wiped his hands on a rag as he rose. Like his brother he stood six feet. In a moment or two he had handed over his usual rent and Barry wrote a receipt.

'I don't think much of your painting, Arthur,' Barry eyed the canvas critically. 'You get worse — if that's possible!'

'At the moment,' Arthur excused himself, 'I've something on my mind.'

'Can only be a woman, I imagine. Anybody I know?'

'You probably do. Jessie Standish.'

Barry looked surprised. 'You mean the Standish garage just outside the village?'

'Uh-huh. Jessie runs the place with her brother Bob.'

Barry Wood nodded. He was acquainted with the girl. She was fairly tall and dark-haired, pleasant enough but with nothing extraordinary about her. She and her brother lived and worked at the garage, the house being attached, and had built it up into quite a profitable business. It rather surprised Barry Wood that Arthur Caldon, with his artistic tastes, could be interested in the girl. He could not resist saying so.

'Just look around you,' Arthur grinned. 'The queerest men and women marry! How many times upon meeting a couple have you not said to yourself: 'I wonder what he sees in her?' Or vice versa. It's like that with me. I like Jessie a good deal. She's the sort of girl who's a bit of a puzzle: never know how she's going to react. That's what I admire in her.'

'And she reciprocates. I suppose?'

'Surely.'

Barry Wood reflected. 'If it becomes serious, Arthur, I have the feeling that Drake won't like it a bit.'

'Of course he won't — and that's one of my reasons for carrying the affair on. I'm looking forward to the chance of tying up the Caldon name with a garage. Naturally, I wouldn't marry a girl with that as the sole incentive, but it's an interesting side issue.'

'And there's absolutely no chance of you and Drake patching up your differences, I suppose?'

'You ask me that every time you come, Barry,' Arthur reminded him. 'And the answer's the same — no chance at all. I wouldn't even live here and pay rent to him if it didn't happen to suit my purpose.'

Arthur Caldon turned aside and from the bureau picked up a curious-looking knife with an extra-long, thin blade.

'Think that antique-collecting twin brother of mine would be interested in this?' he asked. 'I'd forgotten I had it. Been among my stuff for long enough. Picked it up in India when I was there during the war. No use to me but it might be to him.'

Barry examined it carefully but gingerly, holding it near the hilt crosspiece. The hilt itself was smooth-faced and had some odd designing upon it. Apparently the knife was cast in one piece from the tip of the viciously sharp five-inch blade to the rounded end of the hilt.

Arthur added: 'If he's interested he can see it, name a price, and knock the value off the rent.'

Barry Wood shook his head dubiously. 'In his present mood I doubt if he'll even be willing to listen, Arthur,' he said. 'The very mention of your name seems to inflame him these days. But I'll tell him.'

5

Antique Knife

Arthur Caldon's cottage was not Barry Wood's only call that afternoon. He had several other homes to visit in the village but he had dealt with them all by 5.30 and then started his return walk through the hot summer sunlight. He was halfway down the village high street when he ran into Elva emerging from a little teashop.

'Oh!' she exclaimed, starting as he caught up with her. 'It's Mr. Wood again!'

'Coincidence, pure and simple,' he assured her. 'And a coincidence which I welcome . . . Returning to the manor?'

'Well, yes, but — '

'So am I. A journey shared is a journey halved — to murder a well known quotation.'

Elva looked at him doubtfully but there was nothing she could do but accept his company. So they walked together.

'I notice,' Barry Wood said, 'that you are still labouring under the impression that we don't belong to each other's company. You should grow up, Miss Reeves. Convention doesn't mean half as much as it used to, not even in England.'

'It's easier for you to ignore it than me, Mr. Wood,' Elva told him. 'I've my position to think about. If Mr. Caldon were to see us together he'd probably fire me, and I don't want that to happen.'

Barry Wood changed the subject by asking her what she thought of the district. She was too polite to answer truthfully — recalling her feelings when she had had to walk from the station — but she did praise the buns in the teashop where she had stopped for a rest.

'Mother Ballam's buns are the last word,' Barry agreed. 'In fact I — '

He paused and glanced idly behind him as footsteps sounded further down the road. His expression changed. Elva looked, too, and felt her breath come a little faster. A tall, dark-haired man in rough tweeds was striding after them.

'It's — ' Elva stopped. She was not sure

whether it was Drake Caldon or his brother. Nor could she recall the different sides on which the twins parted their hair.

'It's Drake,' Barry Wood said, pausing. 'On his way back from Barrington, I suppose.'

Elsa hesitated, hardly knowing what she ought to do. So she just waited, studying the hard lines on Drake Caldon's face as he came up.

'I gather your hearing must be failing, Barry,' he said, with a cynical twitch to his undisciplined mouth.

'Why should it?' Barry asked.

'I've been following you and — er — Reeves ever since I got off the bus in the village,' Drake Caldon said, and his dark eyes glanced in Elva's direction. 'I find it most unusual to discover my business manager and the parlour maid sauntering along together — and when you didn't respond to my calls I could only assume that you wished to ignore me. Of course, I'm wrong?'

'Of course,' Barry Wood's voice had a flat, grim note. 'I certainly didn't hear you, and I don't think Miss Reeves did either.'

'Perhaps you were too absorbed in each other to be aware of any outside distraction?'

'Look here, Drake — ' Then Barry stopped as Drake turned aside to Elva.

'I'm not blaming you, Reeves,' he said. 'You are good looking and Mr. Wood is susceptible. But I would remind you that I expect perfection from an employee — '

'Perfection!' Barry snorted. 'You've got it on the brain, man!'

'So, Reeves,' Drake Caldon finished, 'please return to the manor — if that is where you are going — and no more will be said.'

Elva went, hazily realizing that she had expected a far greater outburst. Drake Caldon was still looking pensively after her as she went up the road — then his dark eyes snapped back to his cousin.

'Didn't take you long once my back was turned, did it?' he demanded.

Barry Wood shrugged. 'If I choose to make the acquaintance of Miss Reeves in her off-duty time I'll do it! You're not my keeper, remember.'

'I have the feeling, Barry, that you're

underestimating the position,' Drake commented, and began walking forward slowly so Barry was obliged to walk with him. 'You are forced to do as I say in all matters, and you know it.'

'So you're even bringing pressure to bear here, are you?' Barry snapped. 'Can't you ever let up and give me a chance?'

'I can, but in this instance I don't intend to. If you did not wish to place yourself in pawn you should not have committed murder. It ties one down when somebody else knows about it.'

'That was an accident and you know it!' Barry retorted. 'Why do you have to keep bringing it up? You've held it over my head for the past five years and made me obey your every little wish because of it. It's blackmail, and you know it.'

'You say it was an accident that Thomas Clay got a bullet through him. I say it was murder, and the police would too. I was the only witness, so what I say will be credited should the police ever catch up on you. Behave yourself and I'll alibi for you. If you don't I'll turn you in. The police have never traced you and you have settled down comfortably in this remote spot. The least you can do is to be grateful.'

With an effort Barry controlled himself. 'This has got nothing to do with Miss Reeves, anyway,' he objected. 'You can't tell me what to do about her. I have some private life, after all.'

'True,' Drake agreed, with a sour smile. 'Providing it doesn't conflict with my own. I don't blame you for falling for the girl. In fact from the enthusiastic way you described her to me the other night I guessed that already.'

'I like to think she came down the wrong stairs because of an interest in me.'

'That is what I don't like,' Drake replied. 'That's why I gave orders to reprimand her for her action — so you two would not meet in the same way again.'

'For heaven's sake, man, why?'

'I've decided to marry her.'

Barry Wood had just started to recover from the shock of Drake Caldon's statement when they arrived back at the manor. He took the subject up again when they were together in the library going over the affairs of the estate.

'That brother of mine is still paying up, I notice,' Drake commented, studying the rent-returns sheet. 'I wish he'd either default or refuse to pay so I could kick him out.'

'Not very likely with him having part of the inheritance, is it?' Barry asked.

'Afraid it isn't,' Drake sighed, answering his cousin's remark. 'How did he seem? Bitter as ever?'

'Apparently. And he certainly won't patch up the quarrel, whatever it was about. I've never found out what the row was over.'

'Oh, I couldn't stand his constant criticisms of my actions. You know how I like everything ordered and precise — perfection, as near as it can be achieved.'

'I know,' Barry muttered. 'Pretty nearly a mania.'

'It's sign of an orderly mind. Anyway, he and I are direct opposites. I like a drink; he doesn't. I'm a meat-eater; he's a vegetarian. Besides, as a lover of art I objected to his awful paintings. But even if those things could have been forgiven, I certainly would not have anything to do with him now. Not now he's engaged to Jessie Standish.'

Barry said: 'He mentioned that to me today.'

'They've been engaged for six months. She told me that when I called there recently to get some petrol. Think of it! A Caldon marrying a part-owner of a garage!'

'But what about a parlour maid?'

'Elva Reeves has something which Jessica Standish can never have,' Drake broke in. 'She has sheer and fascinating beauty. For that reason she must become my wife.'

With an effort Barry forced the subject into the back of his mind and said quietly: 'Arthur has an antique knife he thinks you might like to buy. If you're interested, he suggested you knock the price off the rent. Not a bad sort of knife as far as I understand them. You could add it to your collection of art objects.'

'I'm not interested. I don't want any

reminders of him, thank you.'

'And I'm to tell him that next time I see him?'

'Tell him what you like. You know how I feel.'

6

Lady of the Manor

Barry Wood, as he went to his bedroom to change for dinner, was still thinking a good deal about his cousin's decision to marry Elva. He had the deep conviction that there was some other reason for the decision. He could not visualize it as an affectionate impulse. Drake Caldon's attitude towards women, if he had one at all, was questionable.

'For a man who raves about perfection it's an impossible situation,' Barry muttered to himself. Elva isn't perfect, even if she's beautiful. Lame foot. Contradicts everything Drake pretends to stand for.'

Elva herself was undisturbed. Upon returning to the manor she had tea with the other domestics and then retired to her room. Elva sat by the window, making plans. How to approach Drake Caldon, how to break down his iron reserve; how to ignore Barry Wood and convince him, against her natural inclinations, that she wished to have nothing to do with him.

Next morning after breakfast, however, Elva found a chance made for her. To her surprise she was summoned to the library, and found Drake alone there, glancing through his morning correspondence.

Elva closed the door and advanced to the desk, waited in respectful silence, watching the sunlight glancing on Drake's shiny thick black hair. At last he glanced up.

'Oh, it's you, Reeves . . . ' It sounded a needless opening. 'I just want a word with you.'

'Yes, sir?'

'Sit down a moment, won't you?'

As she did so Elva wondered what was coming. The break with convention, that she should be asked to sit down by the master of the manor in his own library, was something that secretly astounded her. At least it seemed to suggest that she was not going to be discharged.

'Reeves,' Drake said, gazing at her

steadily, 'I've been thinking a good deal about that incident yesterday, when you and Mr. Wood were out walking together.'

'I assure you, sir, it was — '

'I know. All his fault.' Drake smiled as though he meant to be friendly, 'My cousin is very susceptible to women — especially beautiful women.'

Elva coloured. 'I think that maybe I encouraged him. I talked rather a lot. I know I had no right — '

'You had every right. It was he who should have known better. However, it can't go on, of course.'

It began to sound like discharge after all.

'No, sir, it can't,' Elva admitted.

'I think, Reeves, to make things correct all round, and also preserve my good name, that you should change your position.'

So it had come to it, after all!

'From parlour maid to secretary,' Drake added, and sat back in his chair to watch the effect. It was worth watching, for Elva looked incredulous.

'Secretary, sir?' she repeated.

'That's what I said. I remain convinced that a girl of your looks and poise — I've been watching you more closely than you realize — is wasted as a domestic. Mrs. Carfax tells me that others who applied for the position can be interviewed again, and somebody taken to fill your place. I have a large amount of clerical work here that requires attention. Neither Mr. Wood nor I have the time to deal with it. I'm offering you the position. It should be worth triple your present salary.'

'Triple — ! But I don't know anything about being a secretary!'

Caldon smiled. 'It's absurdly simple as far as I'm concerned. Merely a matter of arranging and filing letters, and a little typing. You can soon learn that. I shan't need shorthand.'

'Well, sir, it's a wonderful chance for me.' Elva's face was brightly eager. 'I'd have loved to have taken up such work long ago, only I didn't have the necessary qualifications. For an office that is, where they're pretty exacting.'

'Of course,' Drake nodded. 'While you learn you will have every leniency. And there is no reason why the master of the manor — or his business manager — should not be seen with the secretary. I shall see to it that everybody knows you have become my secretary. That will safeguard my name — and yours. It's settled, then.'

'Yes sir. It's settled. Thank you ever so much.'

'Not a bit of it! And Mr. Caldon is much better than 'sir', especially from a secretary.'

'Yes, Mr. Caldon. When would you want me to start?'

'Tomorrow morning.'

With the passing of a week in her new position, in which she mastered the not very difficult art of filing, together with the general duties of a secretary — to say nothing of mastering the rudiments of typing — one finger method — Elva had succeeded in convincing herself that her promotion was not a dream. She was with Drake Caldon more or less constantly. He had paid her a month's salary in advance so that she had blossomed out with new dresses, their colour carefully selected to enhance the flaming red of her hair.

From the few letters she typed, Elva gathered that Drake was interested in the export business — diamonds, furs, and other merchandise of a high value. She even wondered now and again if the deals were entirely above board, then corrected her suspicion with the reflection that there was no reason why they should not be.

Of Barry Wood she saw but little, and then it was either in the way of business, or else at mealtimes.

Elva had been secretary to Drake for a month, and become quite efficient when he asked her to marry him.

'I thought,' Elva said, 'that you were a confirmed bachelor, Mr. Caldon.'

'My first name's Drake,' he said, smiling. 'And no man who speaks the truth is a confirmed bachelor. It isn't natural. He might not find the right woman, but he isn't a bachelor from choice.'

'Would you think it old-fashioned of me if I reminded you that you know hardly a thing about me?'

'Very . . . Besides, I don't want to. You're beautiful and you're efficient. I couldn't ask for much more.'

Unconsciously Elva glanced down towards her feet. Drake made an irritable motion.

'You didn't think I bother over an unfortunate trifle like that, do you?' he demanded. 'Maybe it could even be put right?'

Elva shook her head. 'I was born with it. I've always called it Nature's joke. She gave me the face and the figure, and I'm being egotistical in admitting it, but she certainly economized on the leg.'

'That's another thing I like about you,' Drake murmured. 'Your complete frankness.'

'Parlour maid — secretary — lady of the manor?' Elva laughed. 'What is the local gossip going to say about that!'

'Never mind the local gossip!'

7

Victim of gossip

In three weeks Elva and Drake Caldon were married in thc village church and the ceremony was watched by so many villagers and city friends of Drake's that they overflowed the church into the quiet little yard beyond. Barry Wood was best man. An invitation had been sent to Drake's brother to bury the hatchet and take this part, but he had not even troubled to answer.

Parted from Drake for a few moments after the ceremony, Elva came to a sudden halt in the congratulations to find herself facing Agatha Dunwiddy.

'I suppose, young woman, I should congratulate you,' Agatha said. 'I would if I felt there was anything to congratulate you about. Right at this moment I'm more inclined to be sorry for you.'

'Whatever for?' Elva asked.

'Marrying him.' Agatha nodded transiently to where Drake was standing talking to his friends.

Elva's tone was sharp and her colour high. 'He's one of the nicest men ever.'

'Is he really? Until he gets what he wants, I suppose.'

'I don't understand a word you're saying!' Elva snapped, and swung away angrily.

Drake showed no sign of deviation from his earlier good spirits during the honeymoon, which they took in the south of France.

At dinner one evening when Drake and Elva had been returned home about a week, and when Barry Wood was absent, being in the city, Elva said: 'I'm going to your brother's cottage tomorrow, Drake. I think I ought to know my brother-in-law better. You and he seem to have such bitter hatred for each other it doesn't make sense. To me, anyway.'

'Does it have to?' he asked her, more curtly than he had ever spoken since their marriage.

'No, but I'd like to hear both sides.'

Drake reflected and then grinned cynically. 'Peacemaker, eh?'

'Not necessarily, but there's no reason why his quarrel with you should also be a quarrel with me. I don't like hating people for no apparent reason.'

'No apparent reason! Don't I keep telling you the reason? My views and his are utterly opposed.'

'Was there something else? Something you haven't told me?'

'No, there wasn't. Simply our opposed views. I couldn't stand him, or he me. What's more, I'll consider it a personal slight if you go visiting him with a kindly sister-in-law act.'

Just the same Elva went next morning, Drake having left early for business in the city. She found Arthur Caldon busy in the small garden in front of the cottage.

'Hello, Arthur,' Elva greeted quietly, smiling down on him from over the low fence.

He turned in surprise.

'Well, Mrs. Caldon, of all people!' he exclaimed. 'You won't mind if I don't shake hands? I'm covered in oil.'

Elva reflected that his hands were not particularly dirty but she did not press the point. His likeness to his brother was so extraordinary that Elva could hardly credit it. Her eyes strayed to his hair parted on the left.

'You're not seeing double.' He told her dryly.

'I'm perfectly aware of it — and I don't think you've any need to be so confoundedly uncompromising. After all, I'm your sister-in-law now.'

'So I believe. Moved a bit since you were lugging your suitcase at the crossroads, haven't you? Anyway, what am I supposed to do as your brother-in-law? Kiss you?'

'Don't be ridiculous! At the very least you might use my first name instead of treating me as a stranger.'

'Elva, isn't it?' he murmured idly. 'I remember seeing it in the paper after the marriage.'

'Which you didn't attend,' Elva reminded him.

'Why should I?' he asked. 'And what did you marry him for? His money?'

'Do you have to be so objectionable?' she demanded, her eyes flaming.

He considered. 'No. I don't have to, but anybody acquainted with Drake is automatically an enemy of mine — therefore you, as his wife, rank pretty high.'

'Then that must include his cousin, Barry Wood?'

'No; he's an exception. He's browbeaten by Drake, and I can't understand why he puts up with it. The only conclusion I can draw is that he's done something pretty rotten sometime and Drake knows about it.'

'I don't believe it!' Elva declared.

'Please yourself. You've heard what people have to say about Drake: you're also hearing what I have to say about him. We can't all be wrong.'

'I think you can. The more I see of you the more I think Drake did the right thing in throwing you out of the manor. Does this girl Jessie Standish know what sort of a boor she's going to marry? I'm sorry for her.'

She swung away and went back to the lane before she found herself spurred into even more bitter statements. She went back to the manor, got out the small car and drove to the Standish garage.

To her satisfaction it was a tall, dark-haired girl in slacks and blouse who came out. Some few yards away her brother was at work on a car.

'How many — ?' Jessica inquired as she approached. 'Why, it's Mrs. Caldon! I recognize you from the wedding. We were there, you know — Bob and I.'

'Yes, I'm Elva Caldon,' Elva agreed quietly, and Bob, a tow-haired young man with serious blue eyes, came over and shook hands and then went back to his work.

'Four gallons,' Elva added, and seized the interval in which to think.

Jessica put in the gasoline, then went to the driving seat and Elva handed her money.

'I'm glad to know you, Mrs. Caldon,' Jessica said, smiling. 'I'd like to shake hands, if you don't mind the oil?'

Elva smiled and extended a smeared palm. 'Apparently your brother didn't . . . '

'Oh, he wouldn't!'

As Elva shook hands she noticed with passing surprise that Jessica was short a finger, the second on her right hand — There was only a blunted stump.

'I suppose we'll sort of be related soon?' she said, after a moment, and the look in her dark brown eyes somehow gave the impression that she was wondering how her remark would be taken.

'You mean if you marry Arthur?'

'If!' the girl laughed. 'There's no question about it. We're going to be married very soon now. Look for yourself . . .'

Elva shifted her gaze to the engagement ring.

'I'd like to talk to you about — you and Arthur,' Elva said. 'You and I have something in common — both getting warned before being married. I was told that I was making a mistake in marrying Drake —'

'That's not very hard for me to understand,' Jessica said. 'Most people dislike him, myself included, though I have only seen him when he's called for juice.'

'He's simply the victim of malicious gossip.' Elva answered. 'I've proved that for myself. The fault doesn't lie with Drake but with Arthur. I think you ought to know that.'

'With Arthur?' Jessie looked amazed. 'But there isn't a better chap breathing than Arthur. I ought to know. I'm with him often enough — or I was until recently. He's been doing a lot of painting recently so our meetings haven't been as frequent. But to say it's his fault! No! You're utterly wrong.'

Elva gave a serious smile. 'I'm afraid I'm not the type to give a warning very tactfully.'

'You actually mean you're trying to warn me against Arthur?' Jessie asked, commencing to look annoyed.

'Yes. I don't like to see a girl walking into trouble as you are doing. Arthur may seem all right on the surface, but I'd hate to guarantee how he might behave later . . . As an example, he refuses to acknowledge me as his sister-in-law, and he's insulting on top of it. If he can be like that with me he can be with you. Just think it over, Jessie. I'd go to any lengths to save you from being mixed up with him.' Elva pressed the starter and added with conviction: 'He's about the most detestable man I've ever met.'

She did not wait to hear Jessica's reply.

That evening Drake asked her about her visit to his brother.

'Oh, yes, I saw him,' Elva said. 'And I realize how thoroughly people have slandered you around here. I also think that whatever you did to Arthur must have been completely justified.'

Drake smiled. 'I'm glad you understand at last.'

8

Stabbed in the back

Late that evening Jessica Standish had a visit from Arthur Caldon. It was growing dark and the garage had been closed for half an hour. The girl was seated on the rustic seat outside, and in the repair shop, her brother was finishing a repair job by electric light.

A car stopped, and a dim figure alighted, and Jessie realized it was Arthur approaching. He saw her on the rustic seat and came over.

'Well!' she exclaimed. 'Welcome, stranger! I was beginning to think you had forgotten all about me!'

Arthur laughed shortly. 'That's a foolish thing to say, Jessie. As if I could . . . '

'Can't blame me for thinking it,' she objected. 'You leave me alone for such long periods.'

'You just don't understand the soul of an artist, Jessie,' Arthur told her. 'When I get inspired I forget everything — including you. I just go on working.'

'Am I supposed to believe that?'

'Why shouldn't you believe it?'

There was a long silence and it was Jessica who finally broke it.

'You've changed a lot since we became engaged, Arthur. I may as well tell you that I had to do a deal of lying today to keep up my faith in you.'

'Lying? What about?'

'Your sister-in-law, Elva Caldon, was here this morning. She told me that I'm a fool to think of marrying you.'

Arthur laughed bitterly. 'I'd like to know what it has to do with her! If she said that it was plain viciousness because I'd given her a few home truths earlier in the morning. She came to see me, trying to patch up my differences with Drake. I strongly object to peacemakers and I as good as told her so.'

'She said you were most objectionable. I lied and said you're one of the nicest men ever. But deep down I knew that she

spoke the truth. You have become so
— different. Why, Arthur?'

Arthur got to his feet impatiently. 'If
you want to call the whole thing off say so
and be done with it.'

'I don't. I'm trying to be reasonable.
What do you really find important
enough to keep you away from me for
weeks at a time? Where do you go? I've
been to your cottage many a time only to
find you away somewhere.'

Arthur snapped: 'I'm not going to
explain every little thing I do. If you want
to think the worst do so — and be hanged
to you!'

He turned away but the girl's voice
stopped him.

'Arthur, you forgot something.'

He returned slowly. The girl dropped
something in his hand, something that
caught the light from the stars.

'I'm glad I found out in time,' she said
simply.

Arthur said no more. He strode to his
car and drove away. Jessica watched him
go. Then a figure glided out of the
shadows behind her.

'He asked for that, Sis,' her brother said. 'And he's been asking for it for a long time. You did the right thing.'

* * *

Barry Wood returned to the manor around 11 o'clock from London. He freshened up and then headed for the drawing room. Elva was there, absorbed in a magazine.

'Where's Drake?' he asked.

'In the library. Just got back from his constitutional — the nightly wander to the village and back. I think he's waiting to see you.'

Barry went to the library and found Drake at his desk, going through some papers.

'Well, what did you find out?' he asked.

Barry seated himself at the other side of the desk.

'I think, Drake, you'd be well advised to lie low for a while,' he said. 'The sort of deals you are trying to pull are going to bring the law down on your head sooner or later.'

'Certainly there's an element of risk,' Drake agreed. 'Dealing in exports and imports without paying the duty is bound to be dangerous — but I've done it successfully for years.'

'The authorities are in the midst of a big check-up. I've spent all today in London making inquiries. My advice is to do nothing until the clean-up is over. The black market is flourishing so vigorously these days that the police have got to do something.'

Drake grinned. 'What you mean is you don't want to be caught! You're not in the least interested in trying to save me. In fact you'd be glad to see me landed in the clink.'

'Look here, Drake — why did you marry Elva? You don't really love her. You don't love anybody except yourself. Why did you make her your wife and then put yourself through all this effort to convince her that you're a good fellow?'

Drake said: 'I married her, Barry, so that you couldn't. I love making you uncomfortable. You're such a blasted hypocrite — a murderer, pretending to live honestly!'

Barry tightened his lips, opened the door and went across the hall to the drawing room. Drake followed him.

'Business finished?' Elva inquired.

'For tonight,' Drake told her, pouring port into glasses. 'Business itself is never really finished — is it, Barry?'

'I dunno . . . Suppose there must be an end one day.'

'But how cheerful!' Elva admonished. 'What happened? Did a big deal fall through, or something?'

Drake said: 'Look, dearest, suppose we forget all about business deals, eh? Hardly your worry, anyway.'

Drake settled on the sofa and patted the space beside him. Thus invited. Elva sat next to him and his arm went around her shoulders.

He said, grinning: 'Let's make Barry jealous by kissing each other!'

Elva started a little and dislodged Drake's arm. 'That's not very sporting, is it?' she asked.

'Oh, he won't mind!'

'But I do,' Elva said quietly. 'It was only the whim of my emotions that made me your wife instead of his. I don't think it's quite fair to trample on the rejected suitor.'

Drake studied his port. Without looking from it he said: 'I don't know whether that implies an extraordinary sense of values or whether there's something going on between you two.'

'Drake! What a thing to say!'

'Is it? You don't think I don't know that Barry is cow-eyed over you, do you? Or that you chased him until you evidently decided I was a better bet.'

Elva first looked angry and then bewildered.

'Drake, it's so unlike you to talk to me like this . . . Are you trying to suggest that — '

He grinned. 'There's only one thing you're out for, my dear — as much as you can get!'

'Don't you think you've said enough?' Barry snapped.

'Maybe you've something to add?' Drake suggested.

'Just goodnight! And goodnight, Elva,' Barry added in a quieter tone, then he turned and left the room.

Elva said: 'Drake, did you mean all that or did you say it just to annoy Barry? I know you go out of your way to irritate him whenever you can.'

'I meant every word of it. You're out to advance yourself and I don't blame you. I admire your courage. And by the way, if you have been congratulating yourself on making a conquest in marrying me, please remember that I made your battle easy by smoothing the way.'

'Why did you have to do that?' Elva demanded.

'Why? Because I'm in love with you. I love you, Elva, for your beauty, your willingness to take a chance — your downright deceptiveness! There shouldn't be a thing to mar our happiness, providing you behave yourself.'

'Behave myself!' Elva exclaimed, astounded.

He nodded gravely. 'I'm thinking of Barry. If you step out of line I shall know about it.'

Elva did not say anything. For the first

time she was realizing that all the things that had been said about Drake were correct. He was brutal, cynical, overbearing

* * *

Jessica Standish was awakened by what seemed to have been a faint sound — probably a car passing along the main road, or maybe the wind swinging the garage sign outside.

It took her a few moments to make the transition from sleep to wakefulness and become sure. There was somebody in her bedroom. She switched on the bed lamp and gasped as the light flooded on her nocturnal visitor.

'What's the idea?' she demanded, half sitting up in bed and staring, wide-eyed.

'You don't have to talk that loud, do you?'

'But you're in my room! What do you want?'

'Something that won't take very long,' her potential killer replied.

Jessica hesitated, her face terror-filled.

She knew what was coming. Suddenly she twisted in the bed and made a dive to get out of it. She did not succeed. She screamed in anguish as a white-hot pain bit deep into her back under her left shoulder blade. The world came to a stop in a torrent of darkness as her heart was transfixed from the back. She slumped, head and arms dangling over the edge of the bed.

The visitor turned to the window, re-opened it noisily — for entry had been made this way — and climbed out.

In the next bedroom, awakened by his sister's scream and the noise of the window, Bob Standish hurtled out bed and looked outside. He was in time to see the killer dropping.

Bob Standish raced to his sister's room. It did not take him 10 seconds to realize the ghastly thing that had happened. He swung, raced down the stairs and outside. He was just in time to catch the killer at the end of the concrete drive-in.

'Hey, you!' Bob Standish could have been heard a mile away. 'My sister's dead!

Stabbed in the back! It must have been you — '

Bob Standish had the chance to wonder at the attacker's slowness in escaping. Then Standish collapsed helplessly as something smote him hard on top of the head.

9

Black market deals

Drake Caldon switched on the bed light as there came an urgent knocking on the bedroom door.

He said irritably, 'What is it?' Elva awakened slowly, heard Carfax's voice.

'I think we ought to do something, sir. There's no doubt that the cottage is on fire.'

Then she saw Drake standing at the window, pulling his gown into shape, while beside him, also in a gown, was the butler.

'I don't see that it's any business of mine,' Drake said. 'If my brother has been fool enough to set his place on fire he's only himself to blame.'

'But, sir — Surely we ought to call the brigade?'

'There's no need,' Drake said. 'That blaze will be seen by somebody in the village — '

'But suppose Mr. Arthur is there, trapped? We might get to him in time. It's only four minutes to his cottage.'

'Trapped? Don't be a fool, Carfax. Why should he be trapped? If he is, it's his own fault.'

Elva slid out of bed and into her negligée. She crossed the room and stood at Drake's side, looking at the fire.

'Apparently that fool brother of mine has set fire to his place,' Drake said.

'Then what are we standing here for, just watching?' she demanded. 'He may be hurt and unable to escape. Carfax, phone the fire brigade.'

'Yes, madam, but the master said I was not to — '

'And I meant what I said!' Drake snapped.

Elva looked at Carfax. 'How did you happen to know the place was an fire?' She glanced at the clock. 'It's after 2 o'clock. Were you awake?'

'No, madam. I thought I heard somebody throwing something at the window — gravel maybe. So did my wife. I got up to look and I saw the fire. I couldn't see anybody in the grounds outside to account for whatever might have been thrown at the window. So I came straight here. It can only be Mr. Arthur's place. No other buildings lie in that direction.'

'The fire is dying out,' Drake said.

'Somebody else probably has seen it and called the brigade,' Carfax said. 'That might account for it dying out.'

Drake looked at the bedroom doorway as Barry Wood, begowned, came through it.

He said: 'Arthur's place is on fire and you're doing nothing.'

'You don't seem to be doing so much yourself,' Drake commented.

'That's where you're wrong. I've telephoned the fire station.'

'I'm sure you have relieved Elva's mind a lot,' Drake commented. Then he glanced at the butler. 'That's all, Carfax.'

'Yes, sir.' Carfax went.

'Your brother may be hurt — even dead!' Elva said. 'At least he'll need shelter.'

'I'm going to find him,' Barry said.

Drake called after him: 'Don't bring him in here or I'll kick him out.'

Drake went back to bed again, drew the coverlet over him and turned his face away. Elva fought hard with her natural inclinations to find out what had happened at the cottage.

Presently there was a knock on the door.

'What is it?' Drake snapped out.

'It's Barry. May I come in?'

'Why not? The door isn't locked.'

Barry came in and stopped by the doorway. He was carelessly dressed in slacks, sports coat and flannel trousers.

'The brigade put the fire out,' he said. 'But there's no sign of your brother anywhere.'

'Anything else?' Drake asked.

'No — except that the fire chief is wondering why you didn't show up at the fire.'

'Let him wonder.'

Barry hesitated, then with a shrug he turned and went out.

'Satisfied, my dear?' Drake's cynical voice inquired, but Elva did not answer.

She lay thinking and worrying far into the night.

By morning she had come to a decision. She rose and dressed early while Drake was still asleep. Even the staff was not yet on the move. She gathered a few things together into a suitcase, as silently as possible, put on clothes suitable for travelling, and then hurried downstairs to the library where she began to write a letter.

It took her a moment or two to get her thoughts composed enough to put the words down. She wrote:

'Drake:'

'It would obviously be a waste of time for us to try to continue this farce of marriage. I was fully prepared to do my part, but your sudden about-face has shattered all the hopes I ever had that we might have a reasonably happy married life. I realize now that you deceived me when you married me. I mistook you for a much-maligned man. Last night I saw for myself the kind of man you really are. To prolong our life together would only mean making things utterly intolerable, so

I am going away. I shall see my solicitors concerning the possibility of divorce, and — '

Elva stopped writing as the library door opened. Drake was standing there, a dressing gown thrown about his shirt and trousers.

Elva made a movement to pick up the letter, but Drake snatched it from her hand and read it.

'I suppose most newlyweds start off with a darned good quarrel,' he said. 'It's the only way they can find out about each other.'

'Ours wasn't that sort of a quarrel,' Elva said. 'After your insinuations last night, and your behavior concerning the fire at your brother's place — there's nothing more left in common between us.'

'You don't suppose it was easy for me to behave as I did, do you?' he asked.

Elva was surprised, and she could not help showing it.

'You're not trying to suggest that you didn't mean what you said, are you?'

'I didn't mean a word of it — except

concerning Arthur and his confounded cottage. I meant that all right. But the rest, about you and Barry . . . I laid it on thick, on purpose.'

'But what in the world for?'

'I just told you. The only way to find out about each other is to have a rattling good quarrel.'

Elva shook her head. 'It still doesn't make sense, Drake.'

'But it docs!' he insisted. 'You knew the kind of man I am when you married me. I'm still that same man — but I wasn't at all sure of you. I felt that there might be something between you and Barry. That was why I said all those things. If there had been anything you'd have thrown the words back in my face and walked off with him. The way you behaved, finally deciding to ignore him and remain with me in spite of all I'd said, satisfied me. I was mistaken in my suspicions.'

'What kind of a fool do you take me for, Drake? You don't really think I believe a preposterous story like that, do you?'

'It isn't preposterous! Honest! I had to make sure, and I couldn't think of any other way of doing it than by making myself thoroughly objectionable. As far as I'm concerned it's all over and done with. Elva,' he went on earnestly, 'I'm saying that I'm sorry. I'll make it up to you in any way you want.'

'It's my turn to doubt now, Drake,' she said.

'I admit it,' he answered moodily.

'And you'll do anything to prove that you were only 'testing' me?' Elva found the word horribly repugnant.

'Anything.'

'All right then. Find your brother and patch up the quarrel between you. I don't like him myself — what I've seen of him — but I dislike the feud between you still more. Do that, and leave nothing unturned to do it, and I'll believe you. If you refuse me I shall believe that you really meant what you said last night, and I'll walk out. For good.'

'All right,' Drake agreed, though none too willingly. 'But you couldn't have found a harder thing for me to do. I'll go shave and get dressed, and right after breakfast we'll go to the village and make inquiry after Arthur. I'll find him somehow and do what I can to patch things up. You have my word on that.'

'That's good enough for me,' Elva said; then glancing down at herself: 'And I'd better change into something a little less formal.'

Drake picked up her suitcase and went upstairs. At breakfast Barry Wood joined them but said very little. After breakfast, before he went to the library to discuss the day's business with Drake, Barry found himself alone with Elva for a few moments.

'It takes a lot to open your eyes, Elva, doesn't it?' he asked.

'About Drake?'

'Naturally. After the way he carried on last night, I thought you'd walk out on him.'

'I think,' Elva said, 'that he was simply putting on an act, to test me. To find out if you and I really love each other.'

'Listen, Elva,' Barry said, 'Drake never put on an act in his life, unless it was to his own advantage.'

Elva said: 'You'd better go to the

library, Barry. He'll be wondering where you are.'

Barry gave her a long, doubting look and then went. She remained standing by the broad window, frowning.

'I beg pardon, madam . . . ' Carfax had came into the breakfast room and turned to leave again.

'What is it?' Elva questioned him.

'I was looking for Mr. Caldon. There's an Inspector Butteridge to see him.'

'A police inspector, do you mean?'

'Yes, madam.' Memory of a particularly individual parlour maid still clouded Carfax's respect.

'Mr. Caldon is in the library,' Elva told him.

A police inspector? Be about the fire, probably. Knowing what they did about certain black market deals, however, neither Drake nor Barry gave the fire a thought when Carfax made his announcement. They exchanged sharp looks.

'All right, show him in.' Drake instructed; then as Carfax went he added: 'And if there's trouble you keep your mouth shut!'

10

Routine questions

A Tall, loose-jointed man in a shiny blue serge suit came into the room. Over one arm, hanging by the crook, was an umbrella, and in his hand a battered grey soft hat. The first thing noticeable about him was his expansive smile.

The visitor hesitated and looked from one man to the other. Behind him there came a podgy-faced man in police sergeant's uniform.

'I'm Caldon,' Drake said, shaking hands. 'This is Mr. Wood, the estate steward and my business manager.'

'As you are aware, I am Inspector Butteridge. I'm from the Barrington C.I.D.'

'Barrington?' Drake repeated. Barrington was the nearest town to Caldon village. 'But surely the local authorities are dealing with the fire at my brother's cottage?'

'This,' Butteridge said, ignoring the remark and jerking his head, adorned with bristly grey hair, 'is Detective-Sergeant Meadows, also from Barrington.'

Drake motioned briefly and the two men sat down. Butteridge put his umbrella carefully against the desk and rubbed his thin cheeks as if in preparation for a shave. It seemed to have the effect of wiping out his smile, for there was no trace of it when he lowered his hands. His eyes, very small blue points, gleamed brightly as he leaned across the desk.

'I'm here, sir, on an unpleasant errand,' he said. 'And maybe it isn't altogether unconnected with that fire you just mentioned. My mission here is because of — murder.'

Drake gave a start and Barry snatched his cigarette from his lips in surprise.

'Whose murder?' Drake asked, sitting down slowly at the desk.

'A young woman by the name of Jessica Standish.'

'What! My brother's fiancée? Murdered? It's impossible!'

Butteridge rubbed the end of his long,

hooked nose. 'As you may be aware, Caldon village boasts one policeman, who in the ordinary way pursues his occupation as a grocer. Serious matters such as murder are referred to us in Barrington. He sent for me at 10 to 2 this morning to investigate the murder of Miss Standish.'

'I see . . . ' Drake spoke wonderingly. 'Then what — '

The inspector said: 'The Caldon policeman was first summoned by Robert Standish, brother of the murdered woman and joint owner of the Standish garage. P.C. Barker — to give the constable his official designation — found the girl stabbed to death, half fallen out of bed, still in her night things. Fortunately her brother was awakened at the time of the murder, both by her scream and the noise the murderer made in opening the window to make his get-away. Mr. Standish gave pursuit, caught up with the murderer, said a few words to him — and then was knocked unconscious. The murderer, or at least the man whom Mr. Standish encountered, was your brother, Mr. Caldon — '

For a moment there was not a sound in

the library. Drake just gazed as though he could not believe his ears.

'Naturally,' the inspector added, sitting back and rubbing his cheeks, 'this is a grim shock for you.'

'That,' Drake breathed, 'is putting it mildly! Look here, are you sure?'

'Mr. Standish is. He had a good look at the escaping man before being knocked out. It was your brother all right. He made a confounded noise in escaping, and that's sort of odd. Valuable time was lost while Mr. Standish lay unconscious. That gave your brother time to get clear. It looks as if he set fire to his cottage and then ran for it.'

With a noticeable effort Drake got a hold of himself.

'This is ghastly,' he muttered, pressing finger and thumb to his eyes. 'I admit that I didn't have a very high opinion of my brother, inspector — in fact I haven't spoken to him since he left the manor some three years ago. But that he should commit murder — and his fiancée at that — is something I never even thought of.'

'As I understand it, he was a tenant of

yours? His cottage was manor property?'

'That's right,' Drake agreed.

'Why did he take it when you and he had parted on unfriendly terms? Or such was the information Mr. Standish gave me.'

'As far as I know he took it for two reasons — one to be near Miss Standish, and the other because of the housing shortage.'

The inspector mused obscurely over something, looking at the ceiling.

'I believe,' he said, lowering his blue points to look at Drake, 'that you and he are so much alike that it is next to impossible to tell you apart?'

'Even my father had that difficulty,' Drake said. 'The only distinction is that he parts his hair on the left side and I part mine on the right. We are identical twins, even to voices. We differ only in temperament. Arthur has a much less disciplined temperament than I have. Addicted to wild things. But what about my brother? What's happened to him? Are his remains in the cottage ashes?'

'No. I've been there. We are perfectly

satisfied, and so is the fire chief who helped us, that no living person was in that cottage when it was burned down. The solution seems fairly clear. Your brother destroyed it so he would also destroy all clues that might help to trace him. Fingerprints, for instance. But he will be picked up sooner or later. Y'know, sir, I'm in something of a dilemma. This is the first time I have ever been connected with a case that had twins in it. Sort of confuses the issue.'

'How so?'

'Well, he could impersonate you, or you him.'

Butteridge turned slightly to where the sergeant had been taking notes in shorthand. He understood the vague signal given him, and from a pocket took a knife in a cellophane wrapper. The inspector laid the knife on the desk.

'Ever see that before, Mr. Caldon?'

Drake shook his head. 'Never.'

'It killed Jessica Standish.'

Barry said: 'I've seen it before, inspector. It belongs to Mr. Arthur Caldon. He showed it to me one day.' He outlined the circumstances briefly.

The inspector said: 'That establishes for us that the knife is Mr. Arthur's. For motive we have the fact that yesterday he quarreled with Miss Standish to the extent of breaking off their engagement. That was overheard by her brother. The assumption is that sheer viciousness led him to murder her, which was followed up by destruction of the cottage so no fingerprints could be traced or matched with those on the knife. That in turn seems to suggest an impulsive murder, otherwise he'd have taken precautions not to have fingerprints on the knife.'

'Which bears out my remarks that he has a wilder temperament than I,' Drake commented.

The inspector said: 'I understand, Mr. Caldon, that you did not go to the cottage when it caught fire? But that Mr. Wood here did?'

'I had my own reasons for not going, inspector.'

'You obviously must have known about the fire since Mr. Wood went to see what was happening. Did you tell Mr. Caldon of the fire, Mr. Wood, or what did happen?'

Barry said: 'Carfax, the butler, awakened me and then Mr. and Mrs. Caldon. I telephoned the brigade.'

'How did Carfax know there was a fire? I understand it began about 2 o'clock. Is Carfax in the habit of staying awake all night in case he should catch sight of a fire?'

That bland, ever-widening grin came to Butteridge's smooth face and remained there. Somehow Drake found it infuriating. He had made up his mind that the man was a fool.

He said: 'Carfax told me something about gravel having been thrown at his bedroom window.'

'I see. Well, I'll have a word with the butler as I go out. You, Mr. Caldon, did not leave the house all night, and you, Mr. Wood, only went when you knew of the fire?'

'That's right,' Barry assented.

'I'm sorry to bother you with all these questions,' Butteridge apologized. 'Now I'd like a word with Mrs. Caldon, if I may.'

Drake summoned Carfax and gave him the necessary instructions. In the brief interval that followed, Butteridge felt impatiently in his pockets and then scowled.

'No doubt about it, I must be getting old,' he sighed. 'I came without my notebook. Might I borrow a sheet from your scratchpad, Mr. Caldon?'

Drake tore off a couple of sheets and handed them over. The inspector licked the end of a pencil stump, raised a questioning blue orb to the ceiling, then scribbled something down and pushed the notes in his pocket. Then his attention shifted to the door as Elva came in.

The girl shook hands and smiled rather anxiously as the introductions were made. Butteridge glanced briefly at her limp as she moved to a chair. He himself remained standing.

'There's nothing to get alarmed about. Mrs. Caldon. I'm simply engaged in that irritating business technically known as routine questioning. It concerns murder.'

11

The fingerprints

'Murder!' Elva's colour faded a little. She sat listening while Butteridge related the details. By the time he had finished he was seated again, umbrella between his bony knees and his forearms folded on the crook. His beady blue eyes considered Elva with the intensity of a bird of prey.

'Mrs. Caldon, you saw Mrs. Standish yesterday morning. Or so her brother tells me.'

'I did, yes.'

'First I've heard of it,' Drake said, giving her a sharp look. 'What did you go and see her for?'

Elva looked at him. 'I'd just come from seeing Arthur. After the way be behaved toward me I considered it my duty to warn her that marriage to him mightn't be as happy as she was expecting.'

86

Drake shrugged. 'That makes sense, anyway.'

'I gather that you were quite earnest in your warning, too, madam,' Butteridge added. 'Even to the extent of saying that you'd go to any lengths to save her being mixed up with him — Or didn't her brother hear right?'

'Yes, I did say that, but . . . ' Elva paused and frowned. 'What are you getting at, inspector?'

The wide grin returned. 'Just routine questioning. You saw Mr. Arthur yesterday?'

'Yes.'

'And he was not cordial?'

'He went out of his way to be insulting. I reasoned that if he could do that to his sister-in-law he could also do it to his wife. So I sounded a warning.'

Butteridge motioned to the knife in its wrapper on the desk, but Elva shook her head.

'No, inspector. I've never seen it before.'

'Put it away, Meadows,' Butteridge said, jerking his head to the sergeant

— but his eyes remained on Elva. 'About what time did you and Mr. Caldon retire last night?'

'Eleven-thirty,' Drake answered. 'Mr. Wood had already gone.'

'And you were awakened by the butler around 2 o'clock with news of the fire?'

'That's right,' Elva agreed.

'Can either of you prove that you did not leave the bedroom for any length of time?'

Elva hesitated. 'Well, I was asleep. Heavily so. I think I must have dropped off immediately. I don't remember anything until Carfax was knocking hard on the door.'

'Same goes for me,' Drake added.

Butteridge said: 'According to the divisional surgeon and Mr. Standish, that girl was murdered around 1.30 this morning. A little while after that the cottage fire broke out. It would not take your brother more than seven minutes, running, to get to the cottage from the Standish garage. Even less if he used his car — though I hardly think he would because of the noise it would make upon his approach to the garage.' Butteridge mused over a thought.

'Not that he seemed particularly troubled about making a noise,' he muttered; then aloud: 'Well, anyway, his car was in the garage annexed to the cottage at the time of the fire. All that remains of it is twisted steel. Incidentally, the fire was started by petrol, it appears. Two old cans, battered out of shape, were found among the ashes.'

The inspector got to his feet. 'I'll have a word with the butler as I go out,' he said. 'That gravel-throwing business interests me.'

With the sergeant beside him he left the room and closed the door. Elva said:

'Jessie murdered! I just can't believe it! It isn't 24 hours since she was full of life and — Oh, it's awful! And I can hardly believe it of your brother, Drake. Whatever else he is, he didn't strike me as being a murderer.'

'On the contrary, I think he is just the sort of man who would stab a young girl in the back!' Drake commented cynically. 'Not that I'd ever say as much to that inspector — I merely told him that we disliked each other, and that I hadn't spoken to Arthur ever since he left here three years ago.' He gave a shrug. 'After all, he is still my brother . . . '

'The whole affair's ghastly, whichever way you look at it,' Barry muttered. 'I wish now that I'd never admitted I'd seen that knife before.'

Elva looked at him. 'You have seen it before?'

Barry outlined the circumstances. Moodily, he finished: 'I can only assume that Arthur must have gone out of his mind.'

* * *

As he was driven back to police headquarters in Barrington, Inspector Butteridge sat at apparent peace with the world, both hands locked over crook of his umbrella, his gaunt face turned towards the sky as he lolled his head against the leather seat. He was still in this position when Sergeant Meadows stopped the car outside the solid grey building brass-plated as BARRINGTON

POLICE — C.I.D.

'We're there, sir,' Meadows told him hesitantly.

'Blast it, man, I can see that. Why can't you let me have my think out . . . ?' Butteridge squirmed into an upright position and got out of the car. With Meadows behind him, he walked into the building and along the cool corridor to his own office. He put up his battered old hat and umbrella on to the hook behind the door and then settled at his desk and lighted a blackened briar.

Despite a rustic appearance and an almost oafish grin, Inspector Butteridge had abilities that could have put him in Scotland Yard's C.I.D had he desired it. Instead, an intense love for the country-side kept him in quasi-rural Barrington, and made him the best criminal expert for miles around.

'The interesting part,' he said, squinting at his pipe bowl so that he definitely looked cross-eyed, 'is the gravel-throwing performance on the butler's window. Whoever threw gravel knew that the person concerned would be instantly attracted to the fire — which Carfax admits he was. He also admits he couldn't see anybody below when he looked for the source of the gravel-throwing.'

'And no footprints,' the sergeant added.

The inspector scowled pensively. He and the sergeant had both studied the view as they had left the manor. For quite a distance under the windows of the east wing, where lay the servants' quarters, there were wide, undisturbed flower beds. The nearest path was too far away to be a good position from which to throw, and in any case the possibility was cancelled by the tall elm trees blocking the view of the servants' quarters from below.

Butteridge said: 'That leaves either the roof or the windows opposite. They're above the trees. I mean where Wood and Mr. and Mrs. Caldon sleep.'

'You're not suggesting one of them threw gravel?' Meadows asked.

'Oh, I'm just considering this and that. The point is that neither Mr. or Mrs. Caldon was awake until Carfax aroused them. Or so they say. I can imagine one of them telling lies, but not both.'

'That leaves Wood to be considered,' Meadows commented. 'He had no need to disturb anybody. And he admits he's seen the knife before.'

'Motive, motive!' Butteridge admonished. 'We're jumping to conclusions, Meadows, and that's a fatal mistake . . . The thing that also interests me is the twin angle. There is the possibility that Drake could have impersonated Arthur and murdered Jessie. There is even the motive — to prevent her marrying Arthur. Only it's a weak motive. There may have been some other reason, of course, not yet apparent to us. Assuming he did murder her — and I don't propose at this juncture to go into the why and wherefore — there is one thing he can't escape, nor can any other set of twins.'

'Fingerprints?'

'Yes. There's a clear set on the knife hilt.'

'But we haven't got Drake's. That's the worst of the law: we have no authority to take anybody's fingerprints without a conviction.'

'There are ways round the law.' Butteridge was beaming expansively. He took his wallet from his pocket and laid down the sheets of paper that Drake had given him. Meadows raised his bushy eyebrows as he read:

'Everywhere that Mary went the lamb was sure to go. How confoundedly embarrassing!'

'I had to write something,' the inspector apologized. 'Take this sheet to Labs, along with the knife. On the sheets they will find two sets of prints — mine, which they already have, and Drake Caldon's. Find out if Drake's match those on the knife.'

As Meadows reached the door, on his way to the laboratory, the inspector said:

'I wonder why the killer didn't wear gloves? Why he left such a perfect set of prints? A mistake — or deliberate?'

★ ★ ★

The news of the murder left Elva with a definite feeling of tension. Long after

Drake had departed to attend to his business in the city the feeling remained, and she just could not shake it off. She sat in the morning room, thinking, gazing straight in front of her, trying to decide exactly what had happened to the unfortunate Jessica Standish. She could not rid herself of a suspicion that either her husband or Barry Wood was responsible.

12

Underestimated

She went to the library, locking the door on the inside. In here Drake did most of his business; there might be something somewhere to give a real insight as to his character.

The desk drawers failed to reveal anything beyond documents of various kinds relating to various deals, which Elva did not in the least understand. The connection seemed to be with exports. The one thing that puzzled her was a rubber stamp on several invoices, which said 'duty free.'

She looked beyond the bookshelves to where there hung the death mask of Dante. Behind it was the wall safe. She had seen Drake go to it many a time. She pulled the death mask back on its hinges and gazed at the circular steel plate with its combination lock. That her husband was not the type of man to keep a diary she felt sure, but behind that steel barrier there might be something to shed clearer light upon him.

With a nod to herself she began to finger the knob, but she had not the courage to continue. At last she sighed, swung the death mask back into position and left the library.

She went into Barry Wood's room with a feeling of profound self-condemnation. To love a man and wonder at the same time if he has committed murder — and above all to try and probe whatever secrets he might have — this was not a prospect Elva liked. But she felt she had to find out all she could.

There was nothing in the dressing-table drawers beyond what she had expected to find, and the two suitcases and cabin trunk in a corner were unlocked and empty. Neither was there anything in the wardrobe except suits and — Elva paused, staring at the wardrobe floor. There was a steel cashbox there, pushed into a corner. She glanced about her, made sure the bedroom door was locked, and then pulled the cashbox out. It was not particularly heavy, and it was locked.

She closed the wardrobe door, put the steel box under her arm and went to her own room. She locked the door, and tried her keys on the box. One of them opened it, and inside she found a small pile of news clippings. They were dated almost five years previously. Nearly all of them referred to the same subject, but one in particular seemed to sum everything up:

CITY SHOOTING

As yet there are no further developments in the shooting of Thomas Clay, city exporter and financier, who was attacked in his Throgmorton St. office on Monday morning. His assailant is believed to be a man about five feet nine inches tall, very broad-shouldered, and with fair hair. He was seen hurrying from the building and . . .

Elva read through the other cuttings again and finally she came to a Scotland Yard artist's conception of the wanted man, sketched from composites. Elva felt her throat become dry as she found herself looking at a remarkable likeness of Barry Wood.

'And he said he had seen the knife which killed Jessie,' she whispered, staring in front of her.

Suddenly, completely, Barry Wood had become transformed in her mind. She had loved him, trusted him, and now there was this —

Quickly she put the clippings back in the box and turned the key in the lock. Bethinking herself, she polished it all over with her handkerchief and held it in the handkerchief as she carried it back to Barry's room and replaced it in the wardrobe.

What she had failed to notice was that she had put the cuttings back face up, where they had originally been face down.

★   ★   ★

It was noon when Inspector Butteridge got the reports from the fingerprint department. He sat gazing at the knife and scratchpad paper on his blotter, to each of which was fastened a tag.

The tag on the knife said: 'Prints on knife submitted for inspection are plain arch, 10 ridge, and a man's, judging from size. Prints on scratchpad paper, ignoring those of Inspector Butteridge, are 9 ridge twinned loop and do not tally in any particular.'

'Then Drake Caldon didn't do the stabbing, sir,' Meadows said. 'No getting past that.'

Butteridge tightened his lips and scowled. 'Well, it explodes one bright theory I had — that Drake Caldon was making use of his twinship to Arthur. What we have to do now is prove that these prints are Arthur's. If they're not we'll have to start looking for another killer altogether.'

'You haven't overlooked this chap Barry Wood, sir, have you?'

'Overlooked him! Gosh, no. And that reminds me. I've seen that fellow somewhere before, either in a photograph or in the flesh. I'll get in touch with

Scotland Yard and see if they've any dope on him.'

★ ★ ★

Barry Wood returned to the manor in time for dinner. Elva was in the drawing room, and when she heard him enter the house the thought crossed her mind that she was in the house with a murderer who had not been caught.

She heard him go upstairs and wondered why she should feel so terrified of him coming down again.

'Hello, Elva. Drake not back yet?'

'No,' she answered awkwardly. 'Not yet.'

'Can't be too late for me.' Barry threw himself into a chair and lighted a cigarette. He contemplated Elva in rising surprise as she stood silent by the window, her back to him. At last he said: 'Not very sociable, are you? Anything wrong?'

'No, nothing wrong. I've been thinking . . . After all, one can't toss off the murder of Jessica Standish as though it were nothing. Anyway, I can't.'

'I've been thinking about that, too,' he said.

'Well, what conclusion have you reached?' Elva forced herself to talk as she strolled over to where he was seated. She settled on the couch facing him.

'I've reached just one,' Barry said. 'I think you and I ought to get out of here.'

Elva shook her head. 'That wouldn't accomplish anything. It might even look suspicious — running away together after what's happened.'

'Worse things might happen if we stay — especially to you. It's you I'm thinking about, as always. It's perfectly clear to me that you can't see even now what sort of a person Drake really is.'

'He's my husband, Barry, and it's my duty to treat him as such.'

Barry rose from his chair and settled beside her on the couch, and put an arm around her shoulders.

'Look here, Elva, I'm letting you into no secret in telling you that I love you, and I have the hope that you love me. Since this ghastly business with Jessie Standish I feel there's more reason than ever why you should leave Drake. Leave him flat! I'll go with you, look after you — '

With a wrench Elva broke free and got on her feet. Barry was up too in a moment and crushed her to him and kissed her.

'And I'm not apologizing,' he said, as her eyes searched his face. 'I love you and you love me, and if you're confused through a lot of mistaken ideas about loyalty to a man like Drake, then I'm going to change them for you.'

Just then Drake Caldon came into the room.

'Working up an appetite?' Drake inquired, looking at Elva steadily.

As she did not answer, or Barry either, Drake went to the cocktail cabinet and poured himself a drink.

'Any for you two?' he asked. 'Emotion drains the energy pretty severely so I'm told.'

Barry strode forward, his face unusually grim.

'Look here, Drake, there's nothing to be gained any longer by your suspecting things about Elva and I loving each other in secret. We do, and nothing you or anybody else can say will alter it. I'm making no excuses for what you saw when you came in.'

Drake grinned. 'You hardly could,' he said. He turned to Elva. 'Your hair's untidy, my dear,' he commented. 'You'd better fix it before Carfax announces dinner.'

'There's plenty of time yet,' she answered. 'Just as there's plenty of time for you and Barry to change into evening dress.'

'I think,' Drake said, 'that we might as well dispense from here on with the formality of a monkey suit, Barry. It's inappropriate with so many other informal things going on.'

Barry snapped: 'I'm making an end of all this, Drake. I'm taking Elva away from you, whether you like it or not.'

Drake shrugged. 'All right — and good luck to you.'

'But I never said I'd go!' Elva cried. 'Barry asked me to but I wouldn't. After all, I'm your wife — '

'So nice of you to remember,' he answered, 'I find you in the arms of my cousin after being willing to believe that everything I had suspected was untrue. All right, get out and stay out! If you have any notions about getting a divorce you can forget them. I'll never grant it. I'm the injured party, don't forget.'

'I keep on telling you,' Elva said. 'I don't want to go. It's all Barry's idea! How could I help him making love to me?'

'I do not recall any frantic struggle on your part to escape the manly embrace,' Drake commented.

'Say, wait a minute!' Barry caught Elva's arm and forced her to look at him. 'You didn't repulse me when I kissed you. Yet now you don't want to go away with me.'

Elva shook her head despairingly. 'I just don't know what I want. I hardly even know what I'm saying.'

'I want to know where we stand,' Barry said determinedly. 'I'm going — immediately after dinner. Are you coming or not?'

'Of course she'll be coming,' Drake said. 'I wouldn't have either of you in the place after the way you've carried on.'

'Dinner is served,' Carfax announced, entering the room.

Silence. The butler's gaze went over Elva's distraught features but the distant look did not depart from his eyes.

'Thanks, Carfax,' Drake said. They went into the dining room. They were still there when someone knocked on the front door. Carfax paced out and returned to announce that Inspector Butteridge had called.

'To see whom?' Drake asked.

'I understood him to say all of you, sir.'

'All right. Have him wait in the library.'

When the meal was over they went into the library to find the inspector lounging in an armchair, glancing through a volume on criminal mentality — Theodor Reik's *Unknown Murderer*.

'Very interesting,' he said, holding it up.

'I'm glad you find it so, inspector,' Drake murmured. 'I also have *Psychology of the Criminal* by Smith and Ferri's *Criminal Sociology* if you're interested?'

'Have 'em,' Butteridge said, rising and grinning. He returned the book to the shelf and said: 'I'm sorry to come blundering in on you like this but I need a little embellishment on one or two points.'

They all sat down, and the inspector, his head on one side, regarded Drake critically with his tiny blue eyes.

'You will be relieved to know, sir, that I have no longer any cause to suspect you of being mixed up in the murder of Miss Standish.'

Drake gave a wintry smile. 'Why should I be 'relieved'?'

'I led you to think that you might have had the chance to impersonate your twin. Now I'm reassured.'

'By what means?'

Conscious of the unethical method he had used to obtain Drake's fingerprints Butteridge did not answer the question; instead he said:

'Suffice it, sir, that I'm satisfied it's your brother we want. And no effort is being spared to find him . . . But there is a matter of fingerprints to be gone into.

Fortunately there is a clear set of them on the knife, but without comparison they won't tell us much.'

'I'm just wondering, inspector, if you take me for a fool,' Drake told him. 'Your clumsy expedient with the scratchpad paper, for instance. Did you get a nice satisfactory impression of my finger-prints?'

Inspector Butteridge did not prolong the deception for another moment.

'My apologies, sir. I underestimated you.'

13

I promise

'I haven't read all those books on criminology for nothing,' Drake said, nodding to the criminological section on the shelves. 'The law doesn't allow you to take fingerprints without a prior conviction of the person concerned, but various ruses are adopted to get them. I spotted yours right away, and helped you. I'm not holding it against you. Since I had nothing to do with the murder there would have been no point in my withholding my fingerprints, would there?'

Butteridge cleared his throat. 'Well, sir, many thanks for being so co-operative. You'll see then that it is important for me to get comparison prints to match with the knife hilt. Since your brother so completely destroyed everything he possessed I wondered if you happen to have anything of his lying about the manor here? Something he might have forgotten and never reclaimed.'

Drake pondered for a moment or two and then shook his head.

'As far as I know there isn't anything. His room is still as he left it. Never been used since, but since things have been cleaned up quite a deal since then I imagine any fingerprints there might have been will have vanished.'

'A pity.' Butteridge looked absently out of the window. Then: 'You did say, Mr. Caldon, that it was 11.30 when you retired last night? You and Mrs. Caldon?'

'I did say so, yes, and Mr. Wood went a few minutes ahead of us.'

'And before you retired, where were you?'

'In the drawing room, talking.'

'We had some port,' Elva added.

'And you are convinced that neither of you — Mr. and Mrs. Caldon — heard anything until the butler awakened you?'

Drake and Elva merely nodded. The inspector turned and his nearly hidden eyes fixed on Barry.

'And the butler awakened you too, sir?'

'He did, yes.'

'Would you mind telling me, Mr. Wood, why you were so anxious to get to the cottage when you knew from the nature of the fire that there wasn't a thing you could do?'

Barry's mouth tightened a little. 'I had no other reason than to see if I could get help. Had Arthur been anywhere around, without a roof over his head, I had intended bringing him back here — at least for the night.'

'And you had seen the knife before it killed Miss Standish?'

'I told you that this morning,' Barry snapped.

The inspector asked: 'How many of you had met Miss Standish?'

'I'd met her only once — yesterday morning,' Elva said. 'When I warned her about Arthur.'

'I saw her many a time,' Barry added. 'I used to go there for my petrol.'

'So did I,' Drake commented. 'Never took much notice of her until I knew she was going to marry Arthur.'

'Did any of you notice that she had

some peculiarity about her?'

All three shook their heads.

The inspector picked up his umbrella and hat.

'If you don't mind, Mr. Caldon, I'll take a look at that room your brother used to have.'

'Certainly,' Drake assented.

He conducted the inspector upstairs and into a large, airy, well-furnished bedroom. The bed was completely stripped, but the furniture, massive and old-fashioned, was kept in good condition.

The inspector looked into the empty wardrobe, in the archaic ottoman at the foot of the bed, then into the drawers of the dressing table. At one drawer he paused.

'What are these?' he asked.

Drake looked down at two hairbrushes, their bristles interlocked, their backs made of black and white ivory. He gave a slight start.

'Of course!' he exclaimed. 'I clean forgot! My brother left these behind. Matter of fact I think he hardly ever used them. He's pretty untidy in his habits and relies chiefly on a comb.'

Without commenting Butteridge levered them into a big cellophane wrapper, which he took from his pocket. Then he held them as though carrying a bag of candy. Finally he thrust them inside his jacket.

'May be just what I want,' he said. 'There's nothing more likely to get fingerprints than a pair of brushes.'

He opened and shut the remainder of the drawers but there was nothing further.

He remarked: 'I was going to say there isn't anything more,' he said, 'but there is. I'd better tell all three of you together so there's no mistake.'

He went to the library where Barry and Elva were still seated, waiting. Drake followed him in.

'Tomorrow there'll be an inquest on Miss Standish,' Butteridge said. 'I'll have it adjourned pending the close of the police inquiry. I thought you had all better know that for the time being you should remain on hand.'

'You mean,' Drake said, 'that none of us should go away?'

'Exactly. I can't force you to obey the injunction, but of course it is always wisest to co-operate with police orders, isn't it?' Butteridge nodded to each in turn and beamed. 'Well, good evening. Sorry I disturbed you.'

Drake saw him as far as the front door and then returned to the library. Barry and Elva had risen to their feet and they did not appear to have been speaking to each other. Instead they both seemed moodily thoughtful.

'Rather upsets things, doesn't it?' Drake remarked coldly.

'If you mean about Barry going away with me I'm glad it's happened the way it has,' Elva replied. 'I meant what I said, Drake. I don't want to go. I won't go! Oh, I know that you'll never trust me again, that you may even make my life miserable, but I won't go . . . At any rate, not with Barry,' she finished, and looked at him.

'I'm not going to argue,' he said. 'I don't understand your attitude, that's all. Now that this edict has gone forth I can't go either — not just yet.'

114

'When you can go you may be sure I shall not do anything to detain you,' Drake snapped.

'Then you don't object to my staying?' Elva asked quickly.

'I can't change the law,' he said, looking at her. 'It has forced us to become one big happy family . . . '

* * *

Drake's cynical observation that they had become one big, happy family was hardly borne out in the time they spent together in the drawing room. Elva said nothing, seeming to be lost in cogitation — as indeed she was. Barry picked up a magazine and looked through it until he finally made the curt announcement that he was going to his room. Neither Drake nor Elva responded, but the girl's eyes followed him to the door. She felt a thrill of nervousness pass through her. Of course it would not matter if he looked inside his steel box. There was nothing to show that it had been tampered with and she had wiped away all fingerprints.

Drake, who had been smoking a pipe and considering the floor, raised his eyes to look at her. About her there was every evidence of dejection. She was coiled in a chair opposite him.

'Elva . . . '

She glanced up as he spoke. There was even a vague look of hope in her violet eyes.

'Yes, Drake?'

'I've been thinking . . . You're probably not to blame. About Barry making love to you, I mean. I've forgiven you once and I suppose I can do it again. But tell me this: Do you want to stay here because of me, or because you're afraid to go away with him? I can't help remembering that you said you would never leave — not with him anyway! That leaves an opening for you to clear out whenever the mood takes you. We've got to come to an understanding, Elva. If you're liable to walk off there's no sense in trying to patch things up, is there?'

'No . . . ' Elva muttered, without looking up. 'But — but I do want to stay.'

That doesn't sound very convincing.

Then as she did not comment, Drake snapped: 'Why don't you go away with Barry? Granting you had the chance, I mean. It isn't loyalty to me that stops you. In fact, I don't think you give a hang about me. It's simply the money and the position. I knew that from the start, only I hoped that you might change. You have — for the worse.'

'Oh, the whole thing's so confused!' Elva declared hopelessly. 'I did marry you for your money and the position. Remember I have the disadvantage of a lame foot. Many a man has looked beyond me for that reason. When I saw the chance, I took it. But I was prepared to behave as a wife should behave. In return I expected a human being for a husband, one I could trust and believe in. I've never been able to feel that way about you, Drake.'

'Thanks,' he said laconically. 'I suppose your complaint now is that there's no emotional affinity between us?'

'I've the right to complain about that. I'm not blaming you; I'm just pointing it out. Drake, why did you marry me? I've tried to puzzle it out, but I can't.'

'I thought you would be an asset to the manor. A woman is essential in a place like this. I've been sadly disillusioned, though. I should have realized what would happen from the moment I saw you and Barry walking together in the lane. And while we're about it, what is your reason for refusing to go with Barry? You won't go because you're afraid of him. That's it, isn't it?'

As Elva did not answer he reached out suddenly and gripped her arms fiercely, dragged her forward in the chair. For a second or two there was a look of demoniacal intensity in his face such as she had never seen there before.

'Answer me!' he said. 'You're afraid of him! You think he killed Jessie Standish, don't you? And that he might kill you?'

'Drake — my arms — you're hurting — !'

'Answer me, Elva!'

She stared at him and nodded mechanically. Abruptly he released her and got to his feet.

'I thought that was it.' He looked

broodingly down at her. 'But you must have a reason for thinking as you do. Ideas of that sort don't just suddenly occur, especially about somebody whom you think can satisfy your emotional desires. Why do you think such things about him?'

'I — I just do, that's all,' Elva muttered. 'I don't want to, but — Well, I do.'

'Elva, I'm not a fool!' He reached down and jerked her to her feet and held her tightly. 'The time for saying things and meaning something different has gone by as far as we're concerned. You've a definite reason for thinking as you do about Barry. What is it? Is it something he's told you, some clue you've found, or what? You've got to answer me! Don't you realize that any clue, however small, may be the one hint the police need to solve the mystery of Jessie Standish's death?'

Elva tossed the hair out of her face. Her eyes had a bewildered, frightened look.

'You — you mean that is why you want to know?'

'Naturally. What other reason would I have?'

Suddenly Elva told Drake everything. She could not contain it any longer. The confusion in her mind was such that she could hardly think straight. Though she hated every word she uttered she gave the facts from start to finish, beginning with the search of the library and ending with the newspaper clippings. When she had finished she was crying.

Drake released his hold of her and she sank down into the chair again. When he did not say anything she felt surprised. She glanced up to find him looking down at her. There was no smile, only the level gaze at his dark eyes.

'You're right,' he said at length. 'Barry did murder Thomas Clay, the export broker. I saw it happen. I saved Barry from the police.'

'You mean he really is a murderer?' Elva was nearly inaudible.

'Yes. Unconvicted. He knows that I know; that's why he hates me and never misses a chance to blacken my character. He's foul all through, Elva. If in a weak moment he killed you as he killed Jessica Standish — what then?'

'That's what I'm afraid of,' Elva whispered. 'That's why I don't want to go away with him or have anything more to do with him. If only I — I could learn to hate him, too . . . '

Drake sat down on the arm of the chair and gripped her shoulders.

'You asked me why I married you,' he said slowly. 'That was the real reason — so Barry couldn't. I did it to protect you. I've tried in every way I know to find out if your love for him has cooled off, so far without result. I've insulted you, lashed you with my tongue, done everything except come out into the open. It is not easy — or even convincing, without proof — to say that you are in love with a murderer. The fact remains I saw that shooting take place, even though Barry claims it was an accident.'

Elva's expression was spiritless. 'What a hopeless fool I've been. He's got to go from here, Drake, the moment the law allows it.' Elva stopped and then went on in a more urgent voice, 'Maybe we should tell Inspector Butteridge about the press clippings? Maybe you should tell him that you know Barry has murdered somebody and not been caught . . . '

'If the law finds out, all well and good,' Drake answered. 'If it doesn't I'm not saying anything. I'm not the kind of man to hand over my cousin to justice unless justice closes in on him in the normal way.'

Magnanimity was one virtue Elva had not seen expressed very strongly in her husband — emotionally, anyway. Financially he was generous enough. She wondered at his decision but felt in no shape to argue it out for herself.

'Whatever he may so or do from now on, just rely on me,' Drake said quietly. 'I'll deal with him. If I have your promise, that you will never again allow him to take advantage of you, there's no reason why we can't start again — happily, understanding one another.'

'Yes . . . ' Elva looked at him with distance in her eyes. 'Yes, of course I promise . . . '

14

A restless night

Barry Wood sat in his bedroom, in a chair by the window, smoking.

'There's got to be a reason!' he declared to himself. 'Elva never behaved before as she did tonight — not toward me. She loves me, but she's suddenly become afraid of me. One of two causes could account for that — either Drake has told her all about me, which isn't very likely, or she has found out something for herself.'

His gaze strayed to the wardrobe. He got up and went over to it, took out the steel cash box and raised the lid.

His expression changed as he saw the clippings. They were face up. He had put them face down. He distinctly remembered that he had, so any chance snooper would not be instantly attracted to them.

'I often wondered if I was foolish to

keep them here instead of putting them in safe custody in the bank,' he muttered. 'Have to keep them. Might need them for evidence some day.'

He closed the box, locked it, and returned it to the wardrobe. Then, brooding, he stood gazing at the carpet.

'Which explains much,' he breathed finally. 'Can't blame her. Can't blame her a bit. But if she believes that of me . . . '

He stopped. His mind had not been on Elva so exclusively as on the problem of the murder as a whole. Suddenly his eyes widened in excited amazement and he snapped his fingers under the impact of a tremendous realization.

'Stabbed in the back!' he exclaimed blankly. 'But of course! Stabbed in the back!'

* * *

At midnight the light was still burning in Inspector Butteridge's office. He sat at his desk mulling over the various statements he had collected. At a table in the corner, by no means enjoying the lateness of the hour, Sergt. Meadows sat typing the statement to be signed later by the testators.

'As soon as we get the report on those hairbrush prints,' the inspector said, 'we'll have earned 40 winks.'

'Frankly, sir, I can't see that we've got very far,' Meadows said. 'Each statement only seems to make things more mystifying. Why were you so insistent on asking Mr. and Mrs. Caldon and Mr. Wood if they noticed a peculiarity in Jessie Standish? Where was the point of it? They didn't — at least, according to these statements I'm typing.'

'Oh, but they did — only perhaps the peculiarity did not register strongly enough for them to remember it,' Butteridge said. 'What do you recall about that unfortunate young woman?'

'Just one thing,' Meadows said, 'though maybe I shouldn't call it a peculiarity. The second finger on her right hand was missing.'

'Good, good! That's the peculiarity.'

Meadows looked puzzled. 'What does it prove?'

'Blowed if I know yet,' the inspector said. 'Let's call it one of those irrelevant details that I dote on. However, the sight of a defect, however slight, often breeds intense hatred in the mind of a person who is also physically defective. Why? Because the other person is, in a sense, a mirror. When one is normal the reaction is usually that of sympathy; but not if one is abnormal.'

Meadows found it rather hard going to digest this at 10 minutes past midnight but he strove valiantly.

'So,' Butteridge went on, 'I say to myself, Mrs. Caldon has one leg shorter than the other: Miss Standish has one finger missing. Is there something in it? On top of that Mrs. Caldon was anxious to prevent Jessie marrying — as she thought — badly.'

'I see what you mean, sir,' Meadows looked doubtful just the same. 'For some reason, which only a psychoanalyst could explain, Mrs. Caldon killed Jessie, thereby killing two birds with one stone. It stopped her marrying Arthur and it also wiped her out because of her physical defect. But according to Mrs. Caldon's statement, she did not even notice the defect.'

'If you murdered somebody because they had a defect would you admit that you'd noticed it?'

'This,' Meadows said, 'does not explain the fact that Jessie's brother saw Arthur leaving. Besides, could Mrs. Caldon — if she had anything to do with it — have got back to the manor in time to be awakened to see the fire?'

'Sure she could. Using a car, it's only seven minutes, or even less, to the manor. I know it sounds crazy — and probably is — but every possibility has to be considered. None of which will make me call off the hunt for Arthur Caldon, of course.'

Meadows thought for a moment. 'If Mrs. Caldon did have anything to do with it, how did she get back into the manor and even into bed without her husband knowing?'

'They all had wine before retiring. I checked on that. To drug some of it for the right person would not be beyond human ingenuity.'

'And Wood, sir? What about him? I can't help thinking he's a likely suspect.'

'Tomorrow,' Butteridge said. 'I'm going to the Yard and have a look through the M.O. department. I might discover him in the rogues' gallery. I know I've seen him somewhere, and I think it was in connection with something unsavoury. No use me giving the name of Wood to the Yard since it's a distinct possibility that Wood didn't use his own name in connection with whatever I'm trying to remember. Tomorrow morning we'll get the inquest out of the way before lunch, then I'll nip up to London and . . . '

The inspector was interrupted by the arrival of a man from the laboratory with a report on the brushes.

The tag said: 'Fingerprints on hairbrushes submitted for inspection are identical in 27 particulars (the number demanded by law) to those on the murder knife. No trace of hairs on bristles.'

Meadows grinned as he read over his superior's shoulder.

'That settles that, sir! It isn't any longer in doubt that we want Arthur Caldon. Those are his brushes, you say?'

'Uh-huh. So Drake Caldon told me.'

'Very well then. Identical prints on the knife. What more do we want?'

Butteridge did not answer immediately. Getting up, he went to a steel locker and brought out the knife with which Jessie Standish had been slain. He brought it back to the desk, put it down, then studied the photo-enlargements concerning it.

'Meadows, if you were going to stab somebody, how would you hold the knife? Pick it up and show me. We've got all we want from it.'

Meadows picked the knife up and considered, then he held the hilt in a firm grip about midway between hilt crosspiece and the top. His thumb tip pressed on the top of the hilt.

'Like this,' he said, and swung downwards demonstratively.

'Good. To get force behind the blow. Now look at the photograph and see where the prints are.'

The sergeant looked. They showed, according to the fingerprint department statement, the imprints of a finger and thumb, no more, low down toward the hilt crosspiece.

'Funny way to strike, sir,' Meadows said, frowning. 'It looks as though the blow was aimed with only a finger and thumb gripping the hilt. Couldn't get much power that way. Thumb should have been on top of the hilt to press down.'

'True, true.' Butteridge took his pipe out of his mouth and squinted at it. 'Yet the blade went in as far as the hilt crosspiece, driven with a lot of power. Meadows, I'll wager everything I've got — and it doesn't amount to much — that you couldn't drive a five-inch blade into a woman's body, right to the crosspiece, by using a finger and thumb to grip the hilt.'

★ ★ ★

Elva passed a restless night. The mental turmoils of the day seemed to gather themselves into one nightmarish composite which kept her squirming and wakeful most of the night. Not, she noticed, that she seemed to disturb Drake. He slept on, untroubled, and she found time to wonder at his profound self-sufficiency. But he noticed her haggard appearance when he was awake and saw her arranging her hair at the dressing table.

'Bad night?' he inquired.

'Worst I can remember. Hardly shut my eyes . . . ' Elva gave a wan smile through her reflection.

During the dark hours a thought had crept into Elva's mind. Did Drake perhaps know where his twin was, and for some reason was saying nothing? On the other hand, was there the chance that Arthur Caldon might be dead, perhaps even murdered by Barry? Arthur might have seen Barry leaving after the murder and had been silenced, which would account for Arthur's lack of desire to escape when Jessie's brother had caught up with him.

When Drake came in from the adjoining dressing room where he had been shaving, she said: 'Don't you think it queer that that the police don't find Arthur?'

Drake shrugged. 'Maybe.'

'Drake, there's something else,' Elva went on slowly. 'How was it that Jessie's brother saw Arthur if it was Barry who perhaps committed the murder?'

'I've been wondering about that,' Drake said. 'I can only think of one answer. Maybe Barry went there and committed the murder, was seen by Arthur — who had also gone there for some reason — but got away, leaving Arthur to face the music. Arthur hit out and ran for it, burning down his cottage.'

'Why should he?' Elva asked.

'Because of the knife. My guess is that failing to nab Barry, Arthur might have found his own antique knife in Jessie's back, and was then caught by Standish. He saw how bad it might look for him and so cleared out.'

'All of which sounds dreadfully complicated,' Elva sighed.

'I agree, but I'm remembering that Barry is a murderer, whereas, as far as I know, Arthur is not. The other answer is that Barry really had nothing to do with it and that Arthur is the culprit. Frankly I don't know, and I'm about fed up with thinking about it.'

Elva got to her feet and went to the window, opened it and breathed in the fresh morning air. It was a tonic after the stuffiness of the night and the complexity of her thoughts.

'I'll see you downstairs,' she said.

She found Barry in the morning room.

'You're looking pretty washed out,' he commented.

'I know it.'

'Elva, there's something I've got to tell you.'

'For heaven's sake, Barry, don't start again!' she pleaded. 'As far as I'm concerned we're only under the same roof because we have to be. Don't make things more difficult than they are.'

'I've discovered something, which convinces me that you're in danger.'

'You've said that before and it's wearing pretty thin. I'm not interested.'

'Because you think I murdered Thomas Clay?' Barry asked grimly.

Elva's pulses began to hammer and she felt the colour surge into her cheeks. The steel box, about which she had almost forgotten, suddenly returned to her. She hesitated over answering and then Drake came into the room. Immediately conversation ceased, and because the two men had nothing to say during breakfast Elva kept quiet too. After the meal Drake motioned them to follow him into the drawing room.

When Drake had closed the door, he said: 'I thought I'd remind you, Barry, that until you are permitted to leave here, business goes on as usual. You'd better finish those estate accounts today. There's no outside work to be done.'

'Sure you can trust me not to swindle you?' Barry asked.

'I think you've more sense than try any funny business,' Drake retorted. 'I'm going to the city to check up on those details you brought me — concerning the authorities.'

'You'll find that I was right.'

'And you're coming with me, Elva,' Drake added. 'You can shop, as you used to when you were my secretary.'

'Yes!' She had become suddenly eager. 'I'd love that. I'll go up and change.'

'I wish you wouldn't go, Elva,' Barry said, looking at her in an odd way.

'What do you mean by that?' Drake demanded. 'You don't think I'm ever going to trust you alone with Elva again, do you?'

'It's not that, it's — ' A helpless, desperate look came and went over Barry's face.

'I'm going, Barry,' Elva said with quiet firmness — and left the room. Drake followed her, on his way to the library. Barry stared at the closed door with horror in his blue eyes.

15

Arthur's thumbprint

'Thank heaven you rescued me, anyway,' Elva said, looking at Drake as he drove the big car swiftly down the narrow road, which led beyond the village. 'Anything might have happened if I'd been left with him.'

'You'll never be left alone with him again,' Drake answered. 'I'll watch that, Elva. You're mine — all mine.'

The way he said it almost sounded as if he were gloating; then Elva reproved herself for such a silly thought and surveyed the flying countryside.

'You certainly don't lounge along, do you?' she asked, as they hurtled through Barrington in a cloud of dust. 'Ever been caught for speeding?'

'Never. I can't stand dawdling, Elva. Must have speed, and lots of it.'

'You never used to drive this fast, when

I came with you as your secretary.'

He did not answer. Once clear of Barrington he drove still faster.

'That was a sign we just passed,' she told him. 'It said 'Steep Hill — Low Gear'.'

'It refers to Torrington's Slope,' he said. 'I've done this trip more times than I can count.'

Drake swung the big car round a corner, the tires screaming on the gravel, then he pressed hard on the brake pedal as the start of the long, steep Torrington Slope came into view.

'There you are,' he said. 'I know what I'm doing. I always know what I'm doing. Can't crawl about when we've the city to reach. Be all day at the — ' He broke off with a furious exclamation as the car began to gather momentum down the slope.

'What's wrong?' Elva gasped.

'Foot brake! It's broken — ' Drake pulled at the hand brake lever, but that too was useless.

The slope was not a straight one. It twisted and turned down into a valley, ending at a narrow stone bridge crossing s deep river. Drake tried to change to a lower gear, but could not.

Faster — and faster still they went. The bridge swept up to meet them. Drake swung the wheel, swung it back, and struck the offside front wheel against the parapet. The car vibrated horribly, the back slewing round until it hit the bridge's opposite side. Jammed broadside, it halted.

With a look of frozen fury on his face, Drake got out of the car and inspected the damage. Finally be lay on his back, and wriggled underneath the car. When at last be emerged and stood up there was a glint in his dark eyes.

'That was no accident,' he said. 'It was attempted murder! The brake-rods have been hacksawed through, save for a very small section, which broke under pressure. More by luck than judgment we were not even scratched, but it's a wonder we were not drowned or fatally injured.' Drake looked at the river, then his eyes flashed back to Elva. 'Well, do you want any more proof as to the kind of murdering swine your emotional soul mate is?'

'You mean Barry?' Elva's voice was mechanical. She was still quivering.

'He knows I take this route to London. He knew I was going to London this morning. He knows that I am aware that he once committed murder — and he tried to stop you coming with me this morning. Now we know why. With me smashed up and out of the way everything would have been lovely for him — and you. Wouldn't it?'

'You don't have to drag me into it again,' Elva retorted. 'How could I have known what was intended? Do you think I'd have risked my life had I known?'

Drake calmed somewhat. 'No, I suppose not,' he muttered. 'Sorry. I'm edgy after what happened . . . But I'll finish him for this!' he breathed, half to himself. 'I'll tell the police everything I know about him!'

Elva got out of the car and limped round to where he was standing. She seemed to be thinking about something.

'Suppose, after all, it wasn't he?' she

asked. 'His anxiety to keep me at the manor might only have been to try to tell me something. He was trying to do that just before breakfast, only I wouldn't let him.'

'Then who did this?'

'Your brother, maybe.'

Drake pondered for several moments, his eyes on the buckled front wheel and smashed fender.

'Yes, I suppose it has to be considered,' he muttered.

'If it was Arthur it means that he must be somewhere in the neighbourhood, and I think the police ought to know about it. They'll start a thorough search.'

Suddenly Drake's mood changed. 'I don't think we should tell them anything.'

'Why not?'

'Because I'm convinced it's Barry's work — and because I'm not going to start the law hounding my own brother. I feel about him the same way as I do about Barry. They're both my relatives. I just can't put the law on them somehow.'

'Well, I can,' Elva said, looking at him in wonder. 'A girl has been horribly murdered, Drake, and it's more than a possibility that your brother did it — as well as doing this. Even if we're wrong it can't do any harm to report it. The police can at least search.'

'I won't have it,' Drake snapped. 'Understand? You breathe one word about this and you'll be sorry . . . ' He glanced up the slope. 'There's an A.A. box up there. I'd better 'phone for a repair gang to come and get the car out of the way of traffic and give us a lift back to the manor.'

Elva leaned back against the side of the car and watched him go back up the steadily rising road. A frown knitted her brows. Deep in her heart she did not believe either that Arthur Caldon had had anything to do with the accident: it had more or less slipped out unconsciously as an alternative to Barry, who she was always striving to protect.

Barry . . . She could not get him out of her mind, and even now she kept telling herself that his guilt as the murderer of Thomas Clay had not been proved, and that he was directly responsible for the murderous damage done to the car she could hardly credit.

Gradually, as she waited, a change of mood came over her. The confusion that had been upsetting her mind cleared a little. Drake, for all his assertions to the contrary, had been something of a revelation during this ill-starred trip. Brusque, flamingly suspicious, downright brutal in some of his remarks . . . At the manor Barry had wanted to explain something and Elva knew now that perhaps she ought to have let him speak. Perhaps it was only to tell her that he knew she had examined his steel box. He had hinted at that, though how he could have known what she had done she could not imagine.

When Drake came back he said: 'They're sending a truck and a private car for us. I imagine Barry's face will be well worth watching when he finds we're still both alive.'

Elva said nothing.

It was toward 11 when Elva and Drake returned to the manor — to find that Barry was absent.

'Where's Mr. Wood?' Drake asked Carfax.

'I don't know, sir. He went out about 10 minutes after you and the mistress. He did not say to where, or when he would return.'

'All right.'

Carfax retired from the drawing room, and Drake paced back and forth.

'Couldn't be plainer proof than that!' he declared. 'By now he probably thinks we're accidentally killed. He's made good his escape before any awkward questions are asked about the sawn brake controls. I have the feeling,' he finished, coming to a stop, 'that we'll never see him again. Anyway, now I've got you safely home, I'll go on to London by train. It's essential that I go. I don't think you'll be bothered with Barry, but if he should come back I'm relying on you to do the right thing.'

He departed without further words, and Elva considered what she ought to do: then she went up to Barry's bedroom. There was one sure way of discovering if he had left.

In a few minutes she had satisfied

herself. The steel cashbox and Barry's clothes were all in their places. She took the box to her room and opened it. The press cuttings were still there. She did not know why she felt relieved that he had evidently decided not to escape, but she did. And since he had not it was possible that he had not 'fixed' the automobile.

After she had returned the box to the wardrobe she went back to her own room, picked up the telephone and asked for Barrington police headquarters. The desk sergeant answered her question.

'Inspector Butteridge, madam? Sorry, but he's out. So is Sergeant Meadows. They're attending the inquest of Jessie Standish this morning.'

'Oh, of course . . . ' Elva had forgotten it. 'Well, is there any way I can get hold of him at the coroner's court? It's important.'

'You can ring up Barrington 2-7 and ask for the inspector to ring you up when he has a spare moment.'

'Much obliged.' Elva did as she had been instructed and then she sat and waited. Ten minutes later the telephone rang and Inspector Butteridge was on the line.

'Hello, Mrs. Caldon. Something I can do for you?'

Elva gave the facts about the car accident and the sawn brake controls. When she had finished she added anxiously: 'Please don't say anything to anybody, inspector. I mean — particularly my husband. He expressly forbade me to say anything to you.'

'Why?' Butteridge asked.

'He's loathe to say anything which may mean the arrest of his brother.'

'A man as well versed in the law as your husband seems to be, considering all those books on criminology he possesses, ought to know that it's dangerous to try obstructing the police. However, I shan't say anything to him, Mrs. Caldon, unless I'm forced to. It certainly looks as though Arthur Caldon may be somewhere in the district. I'll have every available man start on a hunt for him right away. Thanks for the tip.'

'If anything else should happen,' Elva said, 'I'll get in touch with you.'

'Yes do that — but not until this evening. I'm going to London after the inquest. 'By.'

For a time Elva sat debating what she should do next. She realized that she had tried at an earlier date — when she had come across Barry's press clippings — to find if possible some facts about the man to whom she was married. She had failed. The only other way seemed to be to confide in somebody who was well acquainted with him, and had been over a period of years. As a parlour maid she could tactfully have pumped Mrs. Carfax, or her husband, or the talkative chauffeur — but all that was ended now. She was the lady of the manor.

But there was Agatha Dunwiddy, who had lived all her life in Caldon Village. She could be found at the headquarters of the Woman's Freedom Movement, she had said. Elva felt relieved at the idea of talking to the woman. She was 20 years Elva's senior. She might be able to give some advice in the present tangle.

Elva got up decisively and left the room.

146

She found the headquarters of the Woman's Freedom Movement to be at Agatha Dunwiddy's house. This was indicated by a bill on the bay window.

The angular lady was surprised to see her.

'Mrs. Caldon!' she exclaimed, staring. 'Extraordinary!'

'Is it?' Elva asked, surprised.

'I didn't mean that exactly.' Agatha motioned her into a spotless room and insisted on making tea.

'It's a queer thing,' Elva said, taking the tea and thanking Agatha for it, 'but all the time I've been in the district and at the manor I don't seem to have made any outside friends. You are the only person with whom I feel I have any acquaintance.'

'And that being so you want to ask me something?'

'I — How did you guess?' Elva asked quickly.

'Well, that's what friends are for, isn't it?'

'I feel that I've just got to talk to somebody, or else explode!' Elva declared. 'I've talked to myself and argued with myself until I'm dizzy. I do it by day and I do it by night.'

'Arguing with yourself won't get you anywhere. Shout it to the world! That's my policy.'

'Yes, but it's not always easy to do that. Sometimes you don't know what people may think.'

'Of course it's the murder of Jessie Standish that is bothering you? I'm not surprised! It's bothering me too, in a detached sort of way. All the people in the village are talking about it. The name of Caldon isn't worth much any more, I'm afraid. Not that it ever did amount to anything really worth while,' she finished.

'What,' Elva said, 'has the Caldon family done — apart from the tragic business of Jessie Standish — to get itself into such bad repute?'

'To condemn the family as a whole would be unfair,' Agatha declared. 'The only person who has ruined the name of Caldon is your husband. I say that without reservation and without apology. I admired you for having climbed so high socially. I felt interested, and still am. The tragedy is that you had to pick Drake Caldon, of all people.'

'You're sure you don't mean Arthur, his brother?'

'I do not!' Agatha snapped. 'Had it been Arthur things would have been very different for you, I imagine. Exceptionally nice man — or was until he vanished after the murder.'

'It was hardly the act of an 'exceptionally nice man' to murder Jessie Standish, now was it?' Elva asked quietly.

'Certainly it wasn't — but, where's the proof that Arthur did it? Only a lot of tomfool clues, which the real killer could quite easily have spread around. It's done. I read detective stories.'

'Yes, but you're forgetting that Jessie's brother saw Arthur.'

'He could just as easily have been your husband,' Agatha retorted. 'He'd never know the difference, especially in a dim light. Even I could never tell them apart even in daylight. Arthur did once tell me that he and Drake part their hair on opposite sides, but I'd be hanged if I can remember which. I judge which is which by the differences in temperament. If there is some sour, cynical observation being made, then I know it is Drake. If a generous act is being performed . . . well, Arthur!'

'All of which is utterly bewildering to me.' Elva confessed. 'I met Arthur once just after I was married and he was unbelievably insulting, chiefly I think because I had become his brother's wife. I think he loathes anything his brother does, and heartily detests anybody connected with him.'

'That,' Agatha said, 'I cannot understand. Unless for some reason his temperament has undergone a complete change. I suppose that does happen sometimes.'

'A little while ago you said that Jessie's brother must have seen my husband and not Arthur. That isn't possible, Miss Dunwiddy. For one thing my husband was in bed: we were both awakened by the butler when the cottage caught fire. For another, the police have found out that the killer's fingerprints are not those of my husband.'

'Mmmm,' Agatha said, frowning. 'No wonder you're sleepless, young woman. Anyway, I don't take back a word I've said. I maintain that you are married to a most questionable person. I suppose you think you are the only woman who ever came into your husband's life?'

'Well . . . ' Elva shrugged. 'I've heard lots of things.'

'Then it won't surprise you to know that there have been sundry hushed-up affairs with certain women in the village. There have also been property deals of a very doubtful nature, which if proof were forthcoming, might be directly traced to your husband's sharp practice. These are the things that make his name detestable. On the other hand you will not find anybody showing any dislike for Arthur. At the time he left the manor everybody said he had done the right thing. As one instance of his good nature, look at this.'

Agatha got up and went over to an oil painting in the corner which Elva had already noticed and had difficulty in seeing. Agatha lifted it from its hook and brought it over in its guilt frame. Elva looked at it interestedly.

'Why, it's Thurston Mount!' she exclaimed. 'I thought I recognized it!'

Elva studied it once more. It was not a good painting, but at least it was distinguishable. The ruined castle was there, grey and shattered, with a cloudy sky behind it. In the foreground were a collection of blotchy color spots, which Elva finally decided were girls and boys with a skipping rope.

'Are these children?' she asked in surprise.

Agatha nodded. 'Plenty of children play up near the castle. It's supposed to be a danger spot, but you know what children are. Can't stop them exploring. As maybe you know, Arthur spent a lot of his time at Theston Mount; plenty of views for him to paint. This one is about the best he ever did but unfortunately he ruined it.'

'He did?' Elva surveyed the canvas from various angles. 'How so?'

Agatha pointed to a white whirligig oval patch in the bottom left corner.

'I called on him at his cottage one day,'

she said. 'It was to ask him for his views on marriage as a bachelor, so I could include it in a speech to the Woman's Movement. I admired his paintings while I was there — this one in particular. I confess I did so more from politeness than anything else, for none of his works was a masterpiece. Because I enthused over this one — it was standing in full view on an easel — he picked it up to give it to me. But the paint wasn't quite dry, and it stuck to his thumb. He looked bitterly disappointed.'

'But surely he could have rectified the damage?' Elva asked.

'Hardly. Note where the mark is — just in the lower centre of the rocks. A man with no scruples could have daubed something over the defect and tried to get away with it, but Arthur is not that kind of a man. He just gave the painting away — to me. I mention it merely to show you the kind of a man he is, as I've always knew him to be, anyway.'

Agatha turned away and began to reach upwards to return the painting to its hook. Elva watched her, a growing thought in her mind.

'Would you sell it to me?' she asked abruptly.

With an astounded look Agatha turned. She lowered the painting down again.

'Sell it?' she repeated. 'You can have it if you want. No question of buying . . . But you know what you're doing, I hope? With Arthur Caldon's signature on the corner your husband is not likely to look upon the painting with favour. Besides, I can hardly imagine it as suitable for the manor house.'

Elva laughed with the quickness of excitement. 'Never mind that! Just leave it to me. I'll return it later if you wish? I really only want to borrow it.'

'Well, it does fill the corner,' Agatha admitted.

'All right, I'll return it in a while.' Elva took it from Agatha's hands and propped it beside her chair. Then she asked a question: 'About how long ago is it since this incident with the painting happened?'

'About 18 months.'

'Long before his engagement to Jessie Standish?'

'Definitely. Otherwise I would hardly have asked him for his views as a bachelor.'

'Did you ever see my husband or Arthur together after they had parted at the manor?' Elsa persisted.

'Never. It seemed to me that the cleavage was absolute.'

Elva nodded slowly and got to her feet. She had a very different expression to when she had arrived. Agatha Dunwiddy noticed it, but passed no comment. The reason for Elva's half smile was simple enough. As she left Agatha's, the painting wrapped in brown paper under her arm, Elva was thinking of only one thing: the painting had the thumbprint of Arthur Caldon. Definitely his print. Agatha had seen it made.

16

Dungeon passage

When Elva got back to the manor she found that Barry had returned. He was in the drawing room, apparently awaiting lunch, and was standing at the window looking out on to the grounds. Elva, her hat and coat and the picture disposed of in the bedroom, paused a little as she saw him standing there.

He turned to look at her, but there was no trace of surprise on his features. Either be had discovered from Carfax that she had not been hurt in the automobile accident, or he had seen her coming up the drive and had had time to get his emotions schooled.

'I know what you're thinking,' he said, interrupting her speculations.

'Do you?' She advanced with her slight limp and stopped within a yard of him, her hand resting on the back of the chair.

There was a look in his blue eyes that she had never seen there before. It seemed to be of profound relief.

'Thank heaven nothing happened to you,' he said, and he clearly meant it. 'I've been distracted ever since yon went with Drake in the car. I couldn't concentrate: I couldn't work. I went to the inquest on Jessie Standish. Thought it would take my mind off things. They adjourned it, pending police inquiry.'

'And did it take your mind off things?' Elva asked.

'No. I kept thinking of you.' He passed a hand momentarily over his forehead. 'I kept having a frightful vision of you all smashed up. Had that happened, I was going to go straight to the police and make a clean breast of everything.'

'You realize what you're saying?' Elva asked, in a low voice.

'Of course I do. I tried to kill Drake and there wasn't the opportunity to stop you getting involved without giving everything away. How on earth was I to know you'd go with him?'

'Then you did fix the brake controls?'

'During the night. I knew he had to go to the city today.'

Elva said: 'It was attempted murder, Barry.'

'I know it, and given the opportunity, I'd do the same thing again. It's the only way out for both of us. Drake's too clever for any law to ever catch up on him. The only way out is to act for ourselves.'

'Catch up on him — for what?' Elva asked wonderingly.

He did not answer. Elva sighed and turned away.

'It's not my way to act like you've done, Barry,' she said. 'No matter what Drake may have done, or may yet do — and I haven't a shred of proof that he's done anything yet — I'll not be a party to murder.'

'You found those press cuttings of mine, didn't you?' he asked. He questioned her without anger. There was only deep gravity in his voice.

'Yes, I did.' Her violet eyes returned his gaze frankly. 'There seemed to be so much deception going on I tried a little for myself, chiefly to get a sidelight on you and Drake. On Drake I got exactly nothing: on you, the cuttings. It means that you shot a man, Barry.'

'Which is why you're scared of going away with me?'

'Only natural, don't you think?'

'I didn't mean to shoot that exporter, Elva; it was an accident,' he said. 'Drake knows it was an accident because he saw it happen. I left the building by the front entrance — and was seen doing so. Drake left by the back. We had both called on Thomas Clay on business. There was an argument and he pulled a gun. I jolted it and it went off, shooting him. I ran for it, dropping the gun on the desk. Lost my head completely. Otherwise I'd have had the sense to go out the back way as Drake did. Trust him to keep cool in an emergency. He swore that I'd murdered him. I couldn't prove otherwise. About that time, five years ago, Drake and I were doing quite a lot of business as partners — apart from the estate here, I mean, and I had refused to handle this deal with Clay because to my mind it swindled Clay out of thousands of pounds. It was because of that that the shooting happened. Since that time, I have been forced to do more or less everything Drake tells me.'

Elva asked: 'Why would he tell the police? He was involved in the business as much as you.'

'He'd work it so that the blame would fall entirely on me. That's his way — sly, crafty. Why else do you think he's got dozens of books on criminology in his library? Purely to weigh up how things are done on the lawful side, and the methods criminals use to gain their ends.'

'All of which does not give you the right to try and murder Drake,' she said.

Barry retorted: 'I heard the other day that the authorities are getting pretty close to Drake's fancy game. His arrest will involve me — and conviction for shooting Clay. For another thing, knowing the devil he is, I can't bear to see you tied up to him. Even if killing him did not mean that you'd automatically come to me, I should at least feel that you were free of him. Add to that the fact that my being implicated in the Clay shooting might also give the police ideas about the murder of Jessie Standish, and then you see the spot I'm in! I couldn't see anything else for it but to wipe him out. With him silenced, I'd stand a good chance of getting out of the mess.'

'Barry, whatever you've done, whatever Drake's done, don't ever try anything again like that smash this morning.'

He did not answer.

★　★　★

At 6 in the evening Inspector Butteridge returned to his Barrington headquarters from his London trip. Since either success or failure always left him with the same bland expression, Sergt. Meadows could not tell whether anything worthwhile had developed or not.

'No news of Arthur Caldon yet?' Butteridge asked.

'Not a thing, sir. Following Mrs. Caldon's information we've got all the available men combing the district, but nothing's turned up. He's done a complete disappearing act as any I've seen.'

'So complete, in fact, that I got to wondering on the way to London if there are two Caldons. If Drake and Arthur Caldon might not be the same person.'

'The butler often saw them together, sir.'

Butteridge said: 'I wasn't meaning in the past, but more recently. The two were never seen together after they quarreled. That was assumed to be because of the quarrel. There might be a more significant meaning.'

With some surprise in his voice Meadows admitted the possibility.

'I went to Somerset House while I was in London,' Butteridge added. 'There is a record of both brothers being born — and no death certificate. That proves there are two — or were.'

The sergeant said: 'If Drake killed his brother the body would have been found by this time.'

Butteridge suddenly changed the subject.

'I had a look at the C.R.O. files, Among them is an artist's drawing of a man — made from various composites — who shot an exporter named Thomas Clay five years ago. The assailant was our friend Mr. Wood up at the manor. It must have been in the Police Gazette where I saw him.'

'That,' Sergeant Meadows said, 'is news!'

'So I think. But there's rather a comical side to it — or serio-comic, anyway. Thomas Clay is still alive.'

'Alive! But I thought you said he was — '

'I said 'shot', same as the newspapers said at the time. I did not say 'murdered'. It seems that Clay was rushed to hospital and the bullet was dug out, a fraction above the heart. The police, who had circulated descriptions of his assailant from what information they had been able to gather, waited for Clay to make charges. But he didn't. He said he shot himself, accidentally, so nothing was done. Certain facts the police had brought to light when he was in the hospital proved that he had been engaged in a customs racket. Unfortunately, his accomplices were only referred to as numbers, so they couldn't be traced. But Clay, upon recovery, was thrown in the jug for five years. With good behavior he's due out any day now.'

Meadows said: 'You mean he didn't accuse anybody of shooting him because that might have involved them when, later, he was brought up for the customs offences?'

'Right — but he didn't do it from a sense of honour. He did it, I think, so that when he came out of jail he could collect from the one who attacked him. Apparently, Mr. Wood.'

The desk sergeant came in and said: 'Mrs. Caldon is here to see you, sir. She says it's important.'

'By all means,' Butteridge said, rising. 'Have her come in.'

He held out a welcoming hand as Elva came into the office, a square brown paper parcel under her arm.

'Well, Mrs. Caldon, I won't say that this isn't a surprise. What can I do for you?'

'I'm rather hoping, Inspector, that there's something I can do for you — and therefore for all of us.' Elva put the painting on the desk and took the chair Sergt. Meadows drew up for her. 'I want you to take a look at this.'

She stripped away the brown paper and handed over the painting of Theston Mount. Butteridge took it and held it so that the light from the window fell upon it. Finally he lowered his eye to the corner.

'Because of this print impression?' he asked.

'Yes. You'll notice that Arthur Caldon painted that. And I have it on the very best authority that he did paint it. I was told so by Miss Dunwiddy of the Woman's Movement. Maybe you know her?'

'I have had the experience of meeting her,' Butteridge agreed, rather ambiguously. 'Well, this is splendid — splendid. You're turning into quite a detective, Mrs. Caldon.'

Elva gave a shrug. 'It occurred to me that you have only to check this print — a genuine Arthur Caldon print — with those you have already to satisfy yourself that Arthur really is the murderer.'

Butteridge put the picture down.

'From which I take it that there is some doubt to your mind about the prints we've gathered so far being those of Arthur Caldon?'

'Well, you don't know for certain that they are his prints, do you?'

'We have a pair of brushes that Arthur used and inadvertently left at the manor. They have the same prints as the knife.'

'Oh . . . ' Elva looked as though she were trying to puzzle something out. 'I didn't know that.'

'Just the same, Mrs. Caldon, a third set will be of great value, particularly as we know they are undoubtedly Arthur's. You've been of great service to us.'

'I'd take it as a great favour if you wouldn't mention this to my husband or Mr. Wood.'

'In so far as I can maintain confidence with you, I will,' the inspector promised. 'Unfortunately I can't give a guarantee . . . Off the record, Mrs. Caldon, you sound as though you're afraid of your husband and Mr. Wood. Am I right?'

'Let's just say — uneasy.' Elva changed the subject quickly. 'I suppose you haven't found any trace of Arthur yet?'

'No trace whatever. We now have men searching there — ' Butteridge motioned to the painting.

'You mean — at Theston Mount?' Elva wondered why she had not thought before of such a good hiding place.

'And there is nothing to report so far,' Butteridge finished. 'Since Arthur was in the region of that place such a lot it occurred to us that it's a perfect spot for a hideout.'

'Yes,' Elva said quietly. 'Of course.'

'Tell me something, Mrs. Caldon. Is your husband a tidy man?'

She was astonished, obviously so. 'Yes, he is.'

'Unusually so?'

'Well, you might call it that,' Elva admitted. 'He makes a good deal of trouble for the staff if anything is out of place. He wants everything as near perfect as he can get it.'

'Is he a man who takes much exercise? Sports, games, tennis maybe?'

Elva shook her head. 'His limit seems to be a constitutional each evening — or rather it was until he married me. He doesn't seem to bother so much now. Until that time he took a walk every evening. Why?' she asked, curiously.

'I am a collector of odds and ends,' Butteridge grinned.

Elva did not return to the manor immediately. The new possibility of Theston Mount had a sudden fascination for her. There was still plenty of evening sunlight left, enough perhaps for a casual exploration. If Arthur were hiding there, and the police had missed him, he might listen to her.

She drove the five miles to Theston Mount along a bumpy road. By the time she reached it, it was almost 7 and the grey ruin was flooded in the long, diagonal beams of the sun.

She studied the Mount interestedly as she walked up the rough slope towards it. It had been built in the 14th century. All that remained of it now were the outer walls and the battlements. She stepped into what had once been the main hall and stood watching a group of girls and boys playing hide-and-seek in the ruins.

Elva began to explore, but there was apparently nowhere where anybody could hide, for any length of time at least. All right for children, but hardly for a fugitive from justice.

Suddenly, as she entered a half collapsed archway, which had once led into a big dining hall, she came face to face with a constable. He recognized her.

'Good evening, Mrs. Caldon.'

'I was just having a look round,' she explained.

'Yes, ma'am. That's all right. Think you might find Mr. Arthur Caldon, mebbe?'

'Well, one more searcher helps, don't you think?' she said, and went on her way, tripping over loose stones, until at last the constable was beyond her range of vision and she had come back to where the children were playing. They came scurrying toward her.

'What time is it, lady?'

'It's 10 after 7.'

'Will you play, too?' asked a chubby little girl.

'No, dear. I think not.' Elva gave the child's thick brown hair a gentle stroke. 'I can't run very well, you see.'

One of the boys exclaimed: 'She's got one leg shorter 'n the other!'

Elva was not embarrassed by the childish tactlessness. She changed the subject by asking a question.

'Do you play here often?'

'Often as we can.'

Elva's mind went back to the painting Arthur had made of this ruin whereon a group of children had been depicted playing.

'Can you remember,' Elva asked, 'if any of you were ever painted? I mean, did a man ever paint you into a picture?'

One of the girls replied: 'Not that we know about, lady. But there was a man who used to sit over there,' — she pointed toward the slope with its hard rocky outlines — 'and do a lot of painting. He had an easel and canvas and stool and everything.'

'And he was twins, as well,' added a young boy. Elva looked at him sharply.

'How do you know that?'

'Because we saw his twin once,' the boy replied. 'He came to see him when he was painting one time. They were talking for a long time. Seemed to be arguing. Then the artist gave him some money and he went away.'

'Was this recently?' Elva asked.

'The 7th July.' As Elva looked surprised, the boy added: 'I only remember the date 'cause it was my birthday. My dad bought me some cricket gear, and I came out here to play after my tea.'

'Did he ever speak to you? Or you to him?'

'Once or twice. We used to ask him what he was doing — or what time it was. He was awful nice.'

One of the boys said: 'But what about the time when he got hit on the shin with your cricket ball?'

Elva's interest sharpened. 'Oh? When was this?'

'About a fortnight ago.' The boy grinned. 'He showed us what we'd done. Took the skin off his right shin. He was mad, but he soon got over it.'

'Aw, come on!' complained another of

the boys. 'We've got to go home soon. Let's go an' play prisoners in the dungeon passage where the bobby can't find us.'

The children surged away from Elva, and she stood looking after them thoughtfully. She recalled that Drake had told Inspector Butteridge that he had not seen his brother since he had left the manor some three years ago. She resolved that she would telephone the inspector before she returned home — there was a telephone kiosk on her route back to the manor. The information might be useful to the police in their inquiries. Then she ruminated on the other piece of information she had heard from the children.

Prisoners? Dungeon passage?

She turned and followed the direction they had taken some few minutes before, but when she got beyond the crumbled archway, which led to a boulder-strewn courtyard there was no sign of them anywhere.

Evidently the children knew of some hidden spot that the police had not discovered.

17

Identical prints

Drake returned to the manor before Elva. Apparently be had accepted Barry's disappearance as a permanency, for when he entered the library to find Barry busy with the estate accounts, Drake halted in amazement. Then cold malignancy crossed his face.

'So, you came back, did you?' He slammed the door and strode over to the desk. 'One thing you don't lack is gall, anyway.'

Barry threw down his pencil and glanced up.

'I suppose you're rather backhandedly referring to my effort to polish you off in the car this morning?'

'You even admit it?' Drake exclaimed.

'I can't think why I shouldn't,' Barry shrugged. 'My only regret is that Elva had to endure such an experience. It was intended for you alone, and it was meant to end fatally . . . And, of course,' Barry finished cynically, 'there's not a thing you can do about it!'

'Don't be too sure about that!'

'Say one word about attempted murder — or about the Clay affair — and I'll bring your black market organization down round your ears. It could put you in jail for 10 years.'

Drake lighted a cigarette. 'I'm prepared to risk that to make you smart for this morning's work.'

'All right,' Barry sat back in his chair. 'Start talking and I'll play a trump card. One that I'm sure you'd much rather have taken out of the pack.'

'What are you talking about?' Drake asked.

'Why not expose me to the police and see for yourself what will happen?'

Drake shrugged. 'If you're so sure of this trump card why don't you talk to the police yourself? What's stopping you?'

'The fact that the fingerprints on the knife that killed Jessie are mine. When Arthur committed the murder he had already arranged to blame it on me. Which was why he burned down the cottage, so his own prints would not be found.'

'Your fingerprints?' Drake snatched his cigarette from his mouth and stared. 'But that old fool of a Butteridge has proved them to be Arthur's.'

'Has he?' Barry asked. 'What has he found of Arthur's to give a comparison set of prints?'

'Hair brushes that Arthur left behind. So how do you account for them? They must have your prints as well!'

Barry was silent for a long time and finally asked: 'What sort of brushes were they? Black and white ivory backs?'

'Yes.'

'Then,' Barry said, 'the thing has an explanation. I have a set of black and white ivory brushes — so have you — so had Arthur. All the rooms have identical brushes as far as the menfolk are concerned. Arthur knew that of course. He must also have remembered that he had left his own pair behind. All he had to do was come in the manor here one day

— pretending to be you — at a time when he knew you and I were out of town. He could then put his brushes in place of my own, and his in place of mine. Naturally my prints would be all over the pair that Butteridge found. He knew the inspector would leave nothing unturned to find something with comparison prints — supposedly Arthur's — on them.'

Drake said: 'He shoved the blame on to you very nicely, didn't he? And you can't get out of it, either!'

'I shall remain out of it unless something happens to give the police a genuine Arthur print, which isn't likely. If that should happen they'll start checking up and trick me into giving my prints away somehow.'

Drake said: 'You'll never get away with another stunt like that one this morning, Barry. I'll be too alert. For the moment let's drop the thing and let the police find Arthur. Once they've done that I think we're enough in each other's toils to let things go on as they were, neither of us speaking for fear of the other.'

During dinner, Elva remained silent, not glancing at either Barry or Drake, and because of her disinclination to talk they too remained silent. Drake made it clear, when they returned to the drawing room, that he would have liked to say a good deal but Elva forestalled him by turning up the radio to such an extent he could hardly make himself heard.

At last he got up and snapped it off.

'What's the idea?' he demanded.

'I was endeavoring,' Elva said calmly, 'to make it endurable for the three of us to be in the same room together.'

Carfax entered. 'Inspector Butteridge to see you, sir.'

'Ask him to come in.'

When Butteridge came in Elva gave him an uneasy glance from behind Drake's back. The fear was upon her that he was about to explode something that she would find difficult to explain — the picture for instance, or her telephone call concerning Arthur. Instead Butteridge said: 'Thought I'd drop over with these statements for you to sign.'

He took folded sheets from his pocket and put them on the table.

They signed the statements. Then Drake asked: 'Is there something else you want to know, inspector?'

'Matter of fact there is. Shall we go into the library, Mr. Caldon?'

'If you mean to talk privately, there's no need,' Drake said. 'I haven't done anything that my wife and Mr. Wood shouldn't know about.'

'Good! You said you hadn't seen your brother since he left the manor, didn't you? A matter of three years?'

Drake's colour seemed to heighten slightly. 'I did, yes. What about it?'

'Nothing — except that you were mistaken.' Butteridge said. 'You met him about 5 o'clock on July 7, up at Theston Mount. You talked to him for quite a while.'

'July 7?' Drake frowned. 'That's quite a while ago.'

'Yes,' Butteridge acknowledged. 'But hardly so far as to be beyond memory. Do you think we should still talk openly, or

178

shall we go in the library?'

'I've nothing to hide.' Drake replied, 'and now you mention it, I did see him on that day. It was a Monday. Mr. Wood was away on business, and could not collect the rents as usual, so I did it myself. I went to my brother's cottage, and found him missing. I guessed he would probably be at Theston Mount, one of his favourite haunts for painting, so I went after him. I found him — and collected.'

Elva gave Butteridge a glance of gratitude for remaining silent about her share in the proceedings, then he left the drawing room and returned to the police car waiting in the drive.

'Well, sir?' Meadows inquired, as he started to drive away. 'What about it?'

'Those kids up at the castle were right,' Butteridge answered. 'Drake and his brother did meet. Apparently Drake collected some rent. I can't prove otherwise.'

The inspector fished in his pocket and from the assortment of signed statements picked out Barry's. He held it before him, his head on one side, and chuckled.

'I don't think he guessed,' he remarked. 'Quite a straightforward operation this time — signing his own statement. But he was kind enough to flatten the paper with his hands. The boys can get a print from it, I'll wager. We know by now that the prints on the knife and brushes are identical, but that they do not belong to Arthur Caldon. Nor do they belong to Drake. That only leaves Wood or an unknown. I'll gamble the prints are Wood's.'

'Which suggests him as Jessie's murderer,' Meadows muttered. 'I could believe it better if I could think of a motive.'

'I could believe it better,' Butteridge said, 'if I could think of him as a killer.'

18

You'll disappear

When the inspector had gone, Elva forestalled any further outbursts from Drake by going upstairs to their room and there remained until it was nearing the time when they customarily had a nightcap of wine. With her she took four sleeping tablets and cupped them unseen in her palm.

She came into the drawing room again to find Drake and Barry were absorbed in going over some sheets which she assumed related to matters of business.

'The lady of the manor become tired of her own company?' Drake asked.

'The lady of the manor regrets that she ever became just that,' Elva sighed. 'Serves me right for trying to reach too high.' She stopped before the big mirror over the cocktail cabinet and touched up the coils of her red hair. 'All I came for is my nightcap.'

'We're still here, you know,' Drake commented. 'No matter how we may feel toward each other, wine is still wine.'

She turned and filled two more glasses, slipped the four sleeping tablets into one of them, and set them on the tray. By the time she had finished Drake had come over to her, leaning against the cabinet. His dark, sharp eyes ranged her face.

'When everything comes to be sorted out, you're quite a vicious little thing, aren't you?' he asked.

Elva shrugged. 'Maybe. I'm human enough to want to get my own back, if that's what you mean. The more I think back on the short time we've been married the more I can see that every word you've uttered has been plain deception.'

'You haven't much room to talk,' Drake responded. 'You married me on the same terms. Loving Barry, you chose me because of the money and background, since when you've done nothing but complain about a raw deal. You don't think I'd be fool enough to give you

182

everything a wife wants when I knew your heart was elsewhere do you?'

The sound of Elva's hand slashing across Drake's face sounded extra loud in the quiet room. Drake moved slightly, one elbow on the cocktail cabinet, and gave a grin.

'You're a hard hitter when you like, Elva.'

Trembling with angry reaction, Elva picked up the tray and held it forward. It was essential to her that Drake take the glass nearest him. He did so. Barry got up and came over to take the remaining glass. Elva put the tray down again and picked up her own glass from the top of the cabinet.

None of them spoke.

Finally she put her empty glass back on the tray and left the room, hurried upstairs. Never before had her nerves felt so strained to breaking point.

★   ★   ★

Elva was in bed with a novel in her hand and the table light on when Drake came in. He yawned.

'Ten minutes longer down there and I'd have dropped off. Long time since . . . ' He yawned again . . . 'Since I felt as sleepy as this.'

He undressed with stumbling movements and got awkwardly into bed. He was snoring very quietly.

Elva remained motionless — waiting, listening. So far she had not heard Barry or any of the staff come to bed . . . At last, to her relief, Carfax and his wife, and then the remaining domestics, came up and went past the door. But there was no sound of Barry. Elva glanced at her wristwatch on the bedside table under the light. It was 11 o'clock.

She waited until midnight, wondering why Barry did not come. Drake was fast asleep.

Elva eased herself up gently into a sitting position. There were two things she wanted to do — to see if Drake's right shin had a scar on it left from a cricket ball, which after only a fortnight should still be visible, and she wanted to go to the castle ruin and explore. In no other way, except by insuring that Drake would sleep throughout the night, could she accomplish her purpose and work without fear of discovery. The trouble was Barry. Why had he not come to bed?

Elva reached out gently with her fingers. Drake was lying with his legs bent, the loose bottoms of his pyjama trousers tugged up over his ankles by the pull of the bedclothes. Watching his face intently, Elva drew up the right pyjama leg very slowly and exposed a muscular calf. She craned her neck, but from her position the front view of his shin was hidden.

Quietly she slipped out of bed and glided round it. Then she stopped as Drake muttered something in his sleep and turned over on his face, shifting his feet uneasily until his legs were buried in a tangle of bedclothes. Something warned Elva to go no further — to wait for another chance.

She began to dress silently and swiftly in a brown wool polo jersey and slacks, then taking a flashlight from a dresser drawer she snapped it on, switched off the bedside light, and left the room. The flash extinguished but still in her hand, she crept down the dark corridor and staircase and noiselessly into the drawing room. The sound of deep breathing came to her as she listened.

Switching the flash on, she directed the beam until it settled on an armchair by the window. Barry was sprawled there, fast asleep. In fact it was more of a stupor, and the reason for it was not far to seek, either. On the table beside him was the wine decanter, half empty, and a glass still half full of wine.

A bitter look of contempt crossed Elva's face and she left the room silently. She departed from the house by the back way.

To get to Theston Mount would take some time, but it was safer walking than using the car, the noise of which might easily disturb someone in the house. As far as the two men were concerned she was satisfied that nothing would disturb them for the next few hours.

The police were still on guard at Theston Mount when she reached it.

Slowly, testing every step, she worked

her way to the spot where she believed the children had disappeared during the evening. She glanced about her, then masking her flashlight with spread fingers she began to investigate the ground. For a long time she saw nothing except stone, grey dust, and sprouting weeds amidst the chaos — then, as she was thinking she would have to give up the whole thing as a bad job she came upon an oblong stone with a rusted iron ring imbedded in it.

She noticed that loose stones and rubbish had been drawn over the stone, perhaps by the children to conceal its position. Putting out her flash, she stooped and grasped the ring and pulled. To her surprise, the square was not over-heavy. Age had eroded it to comparative thinness.

Cold, dank air of the underground blew up in her face as she peered into the depths. Lying on her side she reached down and felt something made of metal. A ladder. She felt the rungs carefully.

She began to descend and switched on her flashlight. She saw that the ladder descended for perhaps 15 feet to a stony floor. In a few moments she reached it.

One end of the underground passage, at the point nearest the ladder, stopped short at a massive wall. In the opposite direction it extended for an indefinite distance, obviously man-made at some remote time, while along one side of it were mighty doors of teak with rusty hinges and old-fashioned locks.

In all there were four teak doors, so old the locks had become rusted. Each door was solid and obdurate, but rusty though the locks and hinges were, it did not entirely preclude the possibility that a key might be able to turn the old-fashioned mechanisms.

Three of the doors had apparently not been moved for ages. They were corroded and fixed. The fourth door, however, had been disturbed. Elva felt a thrill of nervous excitement as she discovered this fact. It was the door at the end of the tunnel furthest from the ladder. The flaking of rust around the hinge joints had been torn apart by the movement of the door itself. Her flashlight showed there were no cobwebs inside the lock whereas there were inside the other three.

The door had been moved at some time not very far distant. Elva flashed the light along the tunnel floor, wondering about footprints. She found the dust was churned up in all directions from the hurrying of children. Several of the clearer prints were definitely those of a child. Playing here in the dark?

There had to be an explanation, and when she continued her investigation to the tunnel's end Elva found the answer. It did not end in a blank wall but in a circular opening. She was looking out over starlit farming land. In the distance she could detect the streetlights of a town. This opening was high up the side of a steep slope, half overgrown with weeds and grass and probably hardly visible at all from the outside. But inside it during the daylight hours, would come sunshine — particularly in the evening.

She glanced back towards it with renewed nervousness. It had certainly been tampered with, therefore behind it there might be Arthur Caldon. The thing to do now was surely to tell that policeman of the discovery before Arthur had a chance to slip out.

Turning her back on the starlit view she retraced her way down the tunnel, looked hard at the invincible fourth door, and then began to move on again in the direction of the ladder. She was brought to a stop by a cold, bitter voice behind her.

'Don't go any farther, Mrs. Caldon! It might be awkward — for both of us.'

It was certainly sheer nervous fright and not impulse of will that twirled Elva round. Her torch beam blazed into a dirty face with narrowed dark eyes and unruly black hair. The light encompassed a soiled grey shirt and stained corduroy slacks. Dark shadow showed where beard and moustache had been imperfectly shaved.

'Arthur!' she exclaimed.

'Don't try screaming,' he warned. 'I know there's a policeman on the watch up above. So far he doesn't know about this down here — or anybody else, except those kids — and now you.'

'What do you hope to gain by hiding down here?' Elva asked helplessly. 'For heaven's sake, Arthur, why?'

'Plenty! Once they've arrested and convicted Barry for the murder of Jessie Standish they'll call off the dogs. That will leave me free to get away, right out of the country.'

'You admit that you killed Jessie?' she asked slowly.

'Certainly I admit it, and I'd do it again. Just because I hadn't been able to see her regularly she flew into a rage and gave me my ring back. I won't let any woman do that to me. So I killed her. I'd known for some time that she was cooling towards me and I'd even been planning to kill her and involve Barry as the culprit.'

'Then ever since the murder you've been hiding down here?'

'Behind that fourth door there. I've known about this spot for years. I've explored these ruins from end to end. When I came here, ostensibly to paint, I also brought canned foods and seized my chance to stack them away in that cell there. I brought everything needful, by degrees, even to razor and toothbrush and bottles of water. I've quite a little home down here, prepared long in advance. I got a wax impression of the lock and had a key made by a London locksmith so nothing could be traced locally.'

Forcing her voice to be steady Elva said: 'This can't go on, of course.'

'You mean you don't want it to,' he retorted.

'Oh, what's the matter with you?' she burst out. 'I'm not Jessie Standish! I never did anything to make you hate me!'

'That you are Drake's wife is sufficient. And of course I can't let you go from here.' Arthur's voice had become malignant again. 'That's all you're anxious to do, isn't it? To run — to scream — to tell all the world that I'm hiding here? And then watch the law hound me to a murder conviction.'

Elva took a step back and came up against the tunnel wall.

'What are you going to do?' she demanded.

'Kill you. You'll disappear. The fact that you have gone from the manor won't worry Drake much. He never worries about anything except himself.'

'Arthur, tell me something,' she said urgently. 'Did you ever get hit on the right shin with a cricket ball? Quite recently?'

'Yes . . . ' He thrust out his right leg and, never taking his eyes from her, drew up his trouser. Clearly visible was a half-healed scraping of flesh.

'Satisfied?' he asked laconically.

'Yes. I'm satisfied.' Elva opened her mouth to scream, but he saw what was intended. His hand clamped over her lips and smothered the cry in her throat.

She struggled frantically, tearing at him with her fingers and nails, kicking at his legs, until something crashed down upon her and the universe seemed to explode into bright lights, which blazed away into utter dark.

19

Scotland Yard

Barry Wood stirred lazily and moved an intolerably stiff neck. As he came out of profound sleep it took him several moments to comprehend that he was crouched in an armchair. One leg was cramped; his mouth felt dry and woolly. He opened an eye and beheld pale greyness amidst the drapes across the window.

The clock said a quarter after 6. He left the room silently and went upstairs. After a shower, shave, and change of clothes he felt normal again except for a throbbing in his head, which he could only ascribe to a hangover.

'For the first and last time in my life I must have had too much to drink,' he muttered, reflecting. 'Queer sensation! Don't remember anything beyond just drinking.'

He tried to think things out, and failed. He remembered having taken a second drink at Drake's suggestion, and even a third: but beyond that — ? He shook his head and finally made up his mind to go for a walk. This he did and returned at breakfast time expecting to find Drake and Elva in the morning room. There was no sign of them. He gave a glance round and then summoned Carfax.

'I fancy, sir, they must be sleeping late,' Carfax commented.

'Looks like it . . . ' Barry considered this, then he hurried upstairs and knocked sharply on the door of their room. When there was no response a startled look crossed his face.

'Anybody at home?' he called. 'It's time for breakfast.'

He listened intently and fancied he could hear the sound of deep breathing. Decisively he turned the doorknob an entered the room. In the dim light filtering through the drawn shades he could see a single figure in the bed. Barry looked about him sharply. There was no sign of Elva. Crossing to the window he drew back the shades. Then grasped Drake's shoulder and jolted it sharply.

'Drake! Snap out of it, can't you? It's breakfast time.'

'Eh?' Drake started and turned heavily, blinking.

With an effort he sat up and became blearily aware of Barry staring at him.

'What on earth are you doing in here?' he demanded.

'Waking you up.'

'Where is Elva?'

'She isn't anywhere in the house,' Barry said.

Drake's gaze wandered to the wardrobes, and he got up and yanked open the door of the one nearest him. 'Her clothes are still here, anyway,' he said.

'I don't like it,' Barry said.

'I don't feel one way or the other about it,' Drake shrugged. 'And I don't like your blasted concern over my wife, either! Get out of here and let me dress . . . ' He winced again. 'Wonder what made me sleep like that? I feel as though a truck had hit me.'

'You probably got tight, same as I did,'

Barry answered. 'I woke up downstairs with the port decanter near me. We must have had too much to drink last night, Drake. Or perhaps we were drugged,' he finished slowly. 'It would account for it. I don't ever remember port laying me out flat. Elva mixed the drinks, remember.'

Drake dragged on his dressing gown.

The breakfast gong sounded as Barry prepared to descend the stairs. He took his place at the table and glanced at Carfax.

'Mrs. Caldon isn't in the house, Carfax. She seems to have gone out during the night and not returned — '

'Then that accounts for something, sir,' Carfax broke in. 'I was intending to mention it to the master. The back door was unbolted this morning. I distinctly remember that I locked it myself last night . . . Then where is madam?'

'That's what's worrying me,' Barry muttered. He said no more, however, and applied himself somewhat perfunctorily to his breakfast. After a while Drake appeared and joined him. Drake glanced sharply towards the butler.

'Hear any strange sounds in the night, Carfax?'

'Not a thing, sir. I take it you are referring to the mistress' disappearance?'

'Yes. However, I don't think we need make a mountain out of a molehill. She has a lot on her mind at present and probably went out early for some fresh air. She'll probably return during the morning.'

'Yes, sir,' Carfax murmured.

Apparently satisfied with this explanation, Drake went on with his breakfast, meeting a grim look from Barry every now and again. When the meal was over Barry put his thoughts into words when — at his request — he and Drake had gone into the library.

'I'm not standing for this, Drake,' he said curtly. 'Something may have happened to her, and I'm going to telephone the police.'

Drake pondered for a long moment, then he seemed to make up his mind.

'Not often I agree with anything you do,' he said, 'but this time you're probably right. As her husband, I'll do the telephoning.'

He picked up the telephone and asked for Barrington police headquarters. First the desk sergeant and then Inspector Butteridge came on the wire. Drake told him everything.

'There's just a chance I might be able to do something about this,' Butteridge said. 'She hasn't been seen during the night; that I do know.'

'You do?' Drake looked surprised.

'I have men watching the manor, in case your brother should turn up and try to get in touch with you.'

'Then I'm not over-impressed with their vigilance,' Drake commented. 'It's perfectly obvious that my wife must have slipped out of the house during the night. Why didn't they see her go?'

'I can only assume that she must have done so very stealthily — perhaps by the back way. Only two men were watching and they concentrated chiefly on the front. Constable Walters, who was on duty last night near Theston Mount — in case your brother might be seen around there — distinctly heard somebody or something during the night. He came to the conclusion that it must have been an animal but he reported it this morning when be came off duty. I'm wondering if it might have been your wife.'

Drake's expression slowly changed. 'What on earth reason would she have for exploring Theston Mount?'

'I don't know,' Butteridge responded, 'unless she thinks your brother might be hiding there. We thought the same thing and have covered the ruin from end to end, including a set of dungeons underground. One of those dungeons has been entered quite recently, in case you're interested. The door shows it, and so does the lock. We had a key made by the local locksmith and went in the dungeon recently, but there was nothing there of interest.'

'What has all this got to do with my wife?' Drake asked.

'Just the fact that the dungeon may be your brother's hideout. When we explored he no doubt kept out of sight, but once we had finished he probably returned. If he happened to be around last night when your wife went exploring what do you think he'd do? He wouldn't dare take the risk of letting her tell what she had discovered. Since she hasn't been seen in the locality, I think Theston Mount is our most likely bet. I'll go over there and direct operations myself.'

'I'll join you,' Drake said. 'Be over in the car as soon as I can.' He put the telephone down and looked at Barry across the desk. 'Do I have to repeat everything, or did you gather it?'

'I heard,' Barry answered. 'And I'll come, too.'

Drake looked for a moment as if he were going to raise objections, then apparently he thought better of it. They left the house together and in a few minutes were on their way in the roadster to Theston Mount, Drake at the wheel.

Inspector Butteridge had not yet arrived. There was only one policeman on duty, watching them attentively as they alighted from the car and walked toward him.

'Morning, Mr. Caldon.' The constable gave a salute. 'Anything I can do?'

'The inspector will do that when he

comes,' Drake answered.

Butteridge's car came into view in a few minutes, the sergeant at the wheel.

'This way,' the inspector said. 'There's a stone flag leading to the underground. You stay here,' he added to the policeman on duty.

When Butteridge came to the flat, ringed stone it was firmly in position. Drake looked at it in surprise.

'If my wife went down there, she certainly put that stone back very neatly,' he commented.

'Or your brother did,' Butteridge pointed out. 'He'd hardly leave it on one side so it would attract notice, hey?'

Sergt. Meadows heaved the stone away and pulled a flashlight from his pocket. One by one the four men descended into the tunnel. Daylight was streaming along it from the hole at the other end.

'I thought I knew this ruin inside out,' Drake commented. 'But I never knew this was here.'

Butteridge replied: 'Neither did we until our explorations brought us to it.

There are the dungeon doors.'

He led the way to them, stopping at the fourth.

'Observe this door?' As he spoke he took a huge newly made key, which Meadows handed to him. 'Been used quite a lot. As I told you over the telephone, we knew that much, but despite surveillance we've never had a glimpse of your brother. We've even allowed kids to play in and out of here in the hope they might scare him into view from some hidden spot — but nothing's happened. If your wife is anywhere I'll gamble she's behind this door.'

With a noisy rattle he turned the key and the door grated open on its ancient hinges.

The flashlight beam went up along the walls to the very top.

'Empty,' the inspector muttered.

'Then where is she?' Drake demanded.

'As to that, sir, I'm as baffled as you are,' Butteridge confessed. 'We must have guessed wrong. I even thought we might kill two birds with one stone and find your brother as well.'

Butteridge turned to the three remaining doors, and despite the fact that the cobwebs over the locks proved they had not been budged for years he insisted on opening each one. It took a long time, and a good deal of forcing of the key — which fitted all four locks, it seemed — but it only served to prove that each dungeon was as empty as the fourth. Barry studied the walls in the daylight glowing along the tunnel. Suddenly he gave an exclamation.

'Inspector, what about this?'

Butteridge went over to him and examined the rough stonework. In the harsh surface were imbedded some fibres of dark brown wool.

'Looks as though somebody has rubbed against this — '

'My wife, I'll bet!' Drake exclaimed, looking too. 'She has a dark brown wool polo jersey she wears sometimes. Be just about the right thing for a night jaunt, wouldn't it?'

'All right,' Butteridge said. 'I'll do everything I can to find your wife, Mr. Caldon.'

With that he turned and led the way back to the ladder, and to the surface. He looked at Drake after the stone had been heaved back into place.

'Better leave it to me from here on, sir,' he said. 'I'll let you know the moment anything turns up.'

'Yes, of course.'

* * *

Caldon and Barry Wood were in the drawing room after dinner when Carfax came in.

'Chief Inspector Conroy of Scotland Yard to see you, sir,' he said, looking at Drake.

Drake's expression gave nothing away. 'All right, I'll see him in the library.' As the butler went out Drake shot a glance at Barry. 'Either there is some unexpected news about Elva or else black marketeering has come home to roost,' he said. 'If it's the latter you'll be in it with me; I'll see to that.'

In the library the lanky Yard man greeted him with a grim reserve as he displayed his warrant card. He was a different type to Butteridge — brusque, but polite.

'Well, inspector?' Drake asked, sitting at the desk and pushing across a silver cigarette box.

20

An honest man

Chief Inspector Conroy ignored the cigarettes, sat down, and asked a question.

'I understand, Mr. Caldon, that apart from being a man of independent means, you are also — shall I say, a dabbler in exports? Furs, jewels, and other commodities for which an export license is required?'

Drake lighted a cigarette. 'That's right.' He made his voice sound perfectly frank and affable. 'I'm managing director of the Astral Export Company — '

'With headquarters in Southampton Street. Yes, sir, I know that. I have been there already.'

'Why?' Drake demanded flatly. 'What right have Scotland Yard to poke its nose into my affairs in this fashion?'

'Scotland Yard has the right to poke

into any affair, Mr. Caldon, when it has good reason for thinking that regulations have been contravened.'

'Are you accusing me of shady business?' Drake asked in a grim voice.

'I have to get proof — which I'm sure you won't mind supplying.'

'I will if I can. What exactly do you want?'

'Your accounts for the past five years, together with all bills of trading, receipts, invoices, and manifests.'

'That's impossible,' Drake said. 'You haven't the authority.'

'I can get it,' Conroy said. 'But we don't believe in taking out a search warrant until we're forced. After all, since it is merely to establish your business integrity you can have no purpose in refusing the request. And I'm sure you have been business man enough to keep a record of your transactions.'

Drake adopted a more conciliatory tone.

'I'm sure there has been an absurd mixup somewhere, inspector. You see me. You see my home. What on earth need would I have to get mixed up in illegal trading?'

Conroy was impassive. 'My profession is solely that of studying facts and figures, sir. You are simply asked to co-operate and supply information. And I'm sure,' Conroy finished, getting up, 'that you will. Thank you, sir, and good evening.'

Conroy shook hands and closed the door quietly as he went out. For several moments Drake stood with a deeper colour in his face, then he strode to the door, whipped it open, and called across the hall.

'Barry, come here!'

Barry came and looked questioningly as he closed the door. In savage tones Drake told him what had happened.

'That's bad,' Barry said, shaking his head when he had gathered the facts. 'Infernally bad. Unless you can get a set of books fixed — '

'I have no books. I was careful not to keep any. Even if I had a set and could get a shady auditor to doctor them up the police would find it out. All I have got are a few vital receipts from this year's transactions. Of preceding years I have no trace. I took the risk of destroying everything to save any possible proof for accusation; now I find I need receipts to prove my innocence. Here's all I have.'

Drake pulled open a desk drawer and took out a stack of invoices. Barry had seen them before, stamped 'Duty Free.'

'Better destroy them as well.' he said. 'The exemption stamp is a fake. We don't want to advertise it.'

'They've put me into a corner,' Drake said, banging down his fist. 'No threats, no accusations, no arrest — All I have to do is prove that my transactions have been honest! They know I can never prove that — and when I don't I'll be finished.'

Barry frowned thoughtfully. 'It had to come. It's been brewing for long enough.'

'What I can't understand,' Drake muttered, 'is who gave the police the evidence pointing to me. I don't understand it — unless it was you?'

Barry met the suspicious gaze squarely. 'You must take me for several kinds of a fool. Since I'll inevitably be dragged down in this, why on earth should I wish to start it?'

'Well, somebody's talked out of turn. And it could only be somebody intimately acquainted with our transactions.'

'As to that,' Barry answered, shrugging, 'it could be any of those with whom we've traded, some of the more disgruntled ones perhaps. On the other hand, it is conceivable that the police themselves have been able to blow this whole thing up in our faces. They have subtle ways of getting at evidence. Or maybe it, could have been Elva.'

'Elva!' Drake stared. 'What on earth could she know about it?'

Barry motioned to the invoices on the desk. 'She went snooping around for what she could find out concerning both of us: she told me as much. I don't doubt but that she saw those invoices. They perhaps wouldn't mean anything to her, but if she tied them up with the rumours she's heard about our black market activities, it becomes a possibility that she told the police something.'

Drake picked up the invoices, took

them over to the grate, and set fire to them.

'I don't know what to believe,' he said. 'Somehow I can't think Elva is mixed up in this.'

He left the room. He had barely reached the drawing room before he heard the front door being hammered upon with the heavy knocker. Presently Carfax came into the drawing room and looked about him.

'What is it?' Barry asked. 'Mr. Caldon is in the library.'

'Thank you, sir. There is a gentleman here to see him — and you. He says his name is Thomas Clay.'

The effect of the name on Barry was so paralyzing that he just sat and gaped. Then he got to his feet in a daze. It could not be the same Thomas Clay, of course. Just a crazy coincidence — or maybe his son, or perhaps a relative of the same name. But when he went into the hall and saw the man he knew there had been no mistake. It was *the* Thomas Clay.

He looked a little older, a little greyer,

but otherwise he saw still the same thin-faced, stoop-shouldered exporter whom Barry felt convinced he had shot dead five years before.

'Evening, Mr. Wood,' Clay greeted calmly, holding out his hand as Barry stared at him. 'Bit of a surprise, eh?'

'How do you know my name?' Barry asked, his voice still showing the amazement he was experiencing. 'You never used to know it.'

'There are lots of things I didn't used to know, which I know now.'

The library door was opened and Drake came out, dismissing Carfax briefly. He came striding across the hall, his face darkly troubled from the misfortune that had piled on top of him. He stared at Clay.

'Then it *is* you!' he gasped.

'Yes.' It was Barry who made the answer, with a coldly triumphant smile. 'It's Thomas Clay, all right.'

Drake controlled himself. 'We can't talk here. Come into the library.'

He led the way in and shut the door, motioning to a chair. Thomas Clay seated himself and maintained a composed but rather sinister smile.

'Annoying when the past catches up, isn't it?' he asked.

'Not so annoying for me,' Barry said. 'Ever since that day when I accidentally shot you in your office I have believed myself in danger of being charged with murder. What happened? Where have you been in the interval?'

'Jail,' Clay said laconically. 'As for the shooting, the only reason you were not taken up by the police was because I didn't prefer charges against you.'

Drake could not keep the bitter look of frustration from his face.

'Big-hearted, eh?' he said sourly. 'Just couldn't find it in your heart to give us away?'

'There was nothing big-hearted about it,' Clay assured him. 'I couldn't give you away because I didn't know your names.'

'Then how do you know them now?' Drake demanded.

'That would be telling. I — '

'Now I get it!' Drake exclaimed. 'You found out our names somehow and put the police on our track! A chief inspector has only just left here and we couldn't understand how he came to know so much. You did it, didn't you?'

Clay did not answer the question.

'If you're in a spot, Caldon, it's no more than you deserve,' he said grimly. 'And I mean you, not Mr. Wood here. He was never anything but a tool of yours. I don't bear him a scrap of malice.'

'Nice of you,' Drake sneered.

'That gun I drew was at you, Caldon,' Clay went on. 'I'd have shot you there and then for the raw deal you were handing me. Fortunately Mr. Wood saved me from becoming a murderer, even if I did get the bullet myself. You tried to swindle me out of £50,000, and that's why I'm here tonight, my first night out of jail.'

'You're crazy,' Caldon said. 'The only thing you can do is expose me as a black marketer in a big way, but since the police know about that already it won't be news.'

'On the other hand,' Clay said, 'if you pay me £50,000 — which is rightfully mine, remember — I'll prove that you are not a black marketeer. Should be worth it to you, shouldn't it?'

'How?' Drake asked.

Clay said: 'For safety's sake I had a special set of books made of all my own clients, including you. They were intended as a safeguard in case of sudden inquiry. I had a special auditor to do them and I'll guarantee they'll defy detection anywhere. I've kept those books safely hidden, and since they are still where I put 'em I assume the police didn't find them when they searched my effects. All that is missing in the books is your name — same as all other names. It can soon be put in. If those books were produced in court I think they'd swing a jury in your favour.'

'And what about Wood?' Drake asked.

Clay looked at Barry. 'You'll be indicted as an accessory, Mr. Wood — as manager of the business. But the whole thing will collapse automatically and that will free you.'

Drake sat down at the desk and took a cheque book from a drawer.

'How do I know I can trust you?' he asked.

'You'll have to take that for granted. I've already tried to show you that I'm an honest man in not preferring charges against Mr. Wood.'

Caldon wrote the cheque.

21

I will kill you.

When Clay had gone Drake sat for a long time at the desk, brooding, his hand playing with the pen. At last he threw it down and put the cheque book in the drawer. He suddenly seemed to realize that Barry was seated watching him from the other side of the desk.

'You know, of course, what this does to me?' Barry asked.

'I know. You can do what you like and go where you like.'

'Exactly. You can't blackmail me any more. I've five years of insults, brow-beating, and bullying to catch up on.'

'Oh, shut up!' Drake snapped. 'You've been proven innocent as far as Clay is concerned, but that doesn't exonerate you from all blame regarding Jessie Standish.'

'That's a bit thin, Drake, when the

police are more than sure by now that Arthur did it.'

'Maybe, but they don't find Arthur and pin it on him — any more than they find out what's happened to Elva. By this time I'll wager Butteridge has found that the prints on the knife are yours just as you admitted to me that they were.'

'If that is so, why don't the police come and question me?' Barry asked. 'Or even arrest me?'

Drake shrugged. 'I'm in no mood for arguing.'

'Maybe not, but I am.' Barry's blue eyes had an unusual gleam in them. 'I've mentioned that trump card of mine, Drake — and now I know you no longer have a hold on me I'm going to tell the police all about it. What I want to know is — and what *they* will want to know is: How did you know that Jessie had been stabbed in the back?'

Drake frowned. 'How did I know? Everybody knows it. It's in the paper. General knowledge. Don't talk like a fool.'

'I'm not. On the morning after the

murder, before any news was in the paper Butteridge came here and talked of the crime but he did not once mention that Jessie had been stabbed in the back. Yet after he had gone you said in the hearing of Elva and myself that Jessie had been stabbed in the back. How did you know?'

Drake was silent, starring abstractedly at the blotter.

'The police,' Barry finished, 'might make that question into something plenty awkward for you. I heard it, and Elva too.'

'As my wife she wouldn't be able to testify against me,' Drake said briefly, his mouth tight-lipped.

'True, but my word would carry some weight. There are the makings of a nasty mess in this for you, Drake, and you know it.'

Drake said: 'I assume you're thinking I killed Jessie?'

'You could have taken Arthur's place.'

Drake stared. 'How? When?'

'It's possible that you've murdered him! Your reason for doing so would be twofold. One: because you hated him, and two: because he had become engaged to Jessie and you didn't approve of the approaching union. When Elva came along I believe Arthur had probably been murdered. You could have taken Arthur's place, altered your hairstyle, and dressed in his clothes. Nobody would have known the difference because the quarrel kept you separated. You were never seen anywhere together after that — except once, when you met him at the Mount, about which Butteridge found out. That could have been the last time anyone saw Arthur alive. In which case you deliberately arranged it so you collected rents, including Arthur's, on that day, while sending me away.'

Drake appeared to half stifle a yawn. 'And what did I do then?'

'Disposed of Arthur's body and took his place. A quiet lane, never used by strangers, leads from this manor to the cottage — before it was destroyed. You would never have been seen in your occasional journeys back and forth. Nor had you much reason to appear as Arthur since he was known to wander away from home a lot, painting.

'All this time,' Barry continued, 'there was at the back of your mind the fixed determination to kill Jessie. When I went to the cottage and was shown the knife which later killed her it could have been you I saw and not Arthur. You had only to adopt Arthur's pleasantness to fool me. Even your painting seemed in keeping, only the fact that it was worse than usual was perhaps because you were the artist. You knew the rent day when I would call, of course. Since, as yourself, you were supposed to have gone to Barrington on business, how could I ever guess but what I was talking to Arthur? You turned up later as yourself to meet Elva and me in the lane. You didn't use your car that day: you used the bus. See how it fits in? Then at the cottage you gave me the knife to examine, knowing I'd put fingerprints on it.'

'Clever,' Drake admitted.

'Knowing you would never buy the knife, you made that angle safe. You could have killed Jessie, perhaps holding the knife in such a way that my fingerprints were not blurred, whereas you would probably wear gloves. After the murder you deliberately made a noise and moved slowly so that Jessie's brother would have time to see you and identify you as Arthur. All you had to do then was rush back to the manor here. You probably had a car waiting.'

'Wonderful!' Drake applauded. 'And of course I did all that without awakening Elva and then I set the cottage on fire from a distance?'

Barry was still unshaken in his hypothesis.

'As to the cottage — before setting out to kill Jessie you could have wedged a lighted candle in the top hole of a petrol tin, screening the flame from the windows. When the candle burned down in a predetermined time the petrol exploded and the place caught fire. By then you'd be back home and in bed. You could have thrown gravel at Carfax's window in order to draw his attention to the fire and suggest the presence of a mysterious night visitor. As for the object of the fire — Well, Butteridge guessed it. To destroy all traces of Arthur's own fingerprints . . . As far as Elva's concerned, she didn't awaken because she could have been drugged. We all had wine before retiring, and she said she slept with unusual heaviness.'

Drake's face was expressionless as he asked a question.

'How do you account for the fact that Jessie saw Arthur that same evening before she was murdered, and broke off the engagement? Her brother was a witness to that incident, remember.'

'I'm remembering,' Barry acknowledged. 'I'm also remembering that you used to go for a constitutional each evening about that time. Since you always did it, no special attention was attached to the fact that you were out as usual that evening, the same as any other evening. But I thought about it. I thought about it some more when I realized that of late your constitutionals have ceased — no doubt because they have served their purpose . . . It could have been you who broke off the engagement, thus supplying a motive for the murder that happened later. You deliberately made everybody believe that Arthur committed the crime and that he had deflected the guilt to me. In other words a double-deflection, which made you more or less safe by reason of its very complexity . . . I felt pretty sure I was right until your brother evidently reappeared and attacked Elva. That brings us back to our starting point. You must have seen Arthur somewhere to know about that stab in the back.'

Drake got to his feet. 'I think you're crazy! Why, if I was supposed to be Arthur, did I treat Elva so badly when she tried to be friendly? It was not even consistent with Arthur's character as everybody knew him to be.'

'That,' Barry answered, 'was rather clever. You conveyed the impression that Arthur had changed his nature and become embittered. That made the murder that followed seem believable because Elva thought he was unpleasant. Elva, poor girl, was utterly at a loss to understand the different shades of temperament, which Arthur seemed to possess.'

'Then I murdered Jessie just to stop the

marriage? And that when I had married a parlour maid myself? Be logical, man!'

'There is also an answer to that. You admit you detest imperfection.'

A cold glint crept into Drake's eyes. 'And so I do. What of it?'

'Basically, Drake, you're an egomaniac. You see imperfections in nearly everybody and everything, but overlook the fact that these physical imperfections only arouse you to fury because you yourself have a mental imperfection. There's also the psychological fact that that hatred of imperfection might have led you to commit murder — apart from commonplace motives. Jessie was physically imperfect in that she had a finger missing. I think a psychoanalyst would agree with me that you might kill somebody for so trifling an imperfection as a missing finger. I thought of that answer long ago, which was one reason I told Elva she was in danger. I believe that you married Elva not for her beauty, for love, but for the sole reason that you intended finally to murder her. Because of her physical imperfection of one leg shorter than the other.'

As Drake remained silent Barry added: 'From a person who loathes physical imperfection one would expect a perfect crime. Hence the reason, I think, for a double-deflection of guilt. You see how the police might work it out — but they'd stumble, as I've done, at Arthur's mysterious reappearance.'

'You seriously suggest,' Drake said, 'that I murdered a woman just because she was short of a finger? That I would murder my own wife because of a defective leg?'

'I do — with other motives. You might find the mental urge to destroy imperfection something entirely beyond your control. If somehow my theory should prove to be right in the finish — and there should be an explanation for Arthur's reappearance — or should I find that you have murdered Elva, I'll kill you, Drake.' Barry's voice had become so low Drake could hardly hear it. 'Yes, I'll kill you, and do the world a service.'

Drake said nothing. Then suddenly his

right fist came up with devastating power.

'You lying swine — !'

Barry took the blow under the jaw. It hurled him out of his chair and backward on to the floor. When he had staggered up again, cradling his chin in his palm, Drake had gone and the library door was closed.

★ ★ ★

Barry did not see Drake for the remainder of the evening. He assumed that he had gone up to the bedroom — and he was right. Drake was there, but not in bed. He was pacing up and down restlessly. A long succession of shocks and finally Barry's carefully worked-out hypothesis had left him with a haggard face and taut lips. He wondered if Barry would carry out his intention and pass on his ideas to the police. Barry did not, for the chief reason that he was not at all sure himself how much was true and how much he had imagined.

At intervals Drake ceased his pacing and threw himself into a chair to brood, only to find stillness even more harrowing and so he resumed his prowling. The twilight faded and night came. He heard Barry and the domestics come up to bed. He remained silent — and finally reached a decision.

Towards midnight he took an automatic pistol from a dresser draw and slipped it into his pocket, and left the manor by the back way. As quickly as possible he walked to Theston Mount and began to circumnavigate the ruin cautiously in the darkness. wary of attracting the attention of any police who might still be in guard. Picking his way, he finally reached the position where the grassy site of the castle plunged downward into the valley. Sliding over the edge he worked his way down until he had reached the opening in the cliff face which led into the dungeon tunnel. For several moments he remained motionless, then pulling a small flashlight from his pocket he began a silent advance. The tunnel was mildewed and empty.

Pulling his wallet from his pocket, he

took out a large key and slipped it in the lock of the fourth door, turning the lock as noiselessly as he could. Quietly he entered the dungeons, leaving the door wide in case he needed to suddenly depart. He flashed the torch-beam on the right-hand wall, then going over to the far corner he began to pull down the loose stones, which were poised dangerously at the top.

Finally, so laborious was the work, he put down his torch with the beam angled upwards and began to work with ever increasing energy, perspiration pouring down his face. The stones came away easily, piled as they were on top of each other to present the appearance of an age-eaten wall. In half an hour he had stripped a considerable area free, revealing beyond a cavity two feet wide at the back of which was the densely thick wall of the cell beyond.

Taking up his torch again, he began an urgent search of the cavity, flashing the beam into every corner.

'Looking for your brother, Mr. Caldon?' a quiet voice inquired.

Drake whipped the flashlight beam round. Inspector Butteridge was lounging in the doorway, umbrella hooked on his arm and his old hat on the back of his head.

22

Better to forget

Drake was only transfixed with shock for a moment, then his hand whipped down to his pocket and jerked out the automatic — only he was not quite soon enough. Butteridge's umbrella lashed out and struck Drake violently across the wrist and sent the gun spinning. Butteridge picked it up and slipped it in his own pocket.

'Sorry,' he apologized. 'Since the law forbids us police to routinely carry a gun I use an umbrella. I'm quite an expert with it.'

Drake breathed hard. The torchlight was sideways to both him and the inspector so they could dimly see each other. Butteridge gave his slow smile.

'Y'know, Caldon, in all this business you've made the one capital mistake of under-estimating your opponent — as I intended you should. From my manner you assumed — as many people have assumed before to their cost — that I am a brainless villager. I'm not. I have you tied up not only in knots, but there are bows on 'em as well!'

Drake shouted: 'You haven't a thing on me! Not an atom of proof!'

'I haven't? Then what are you here for? Searching for birds' nests? How did you get in when you're not supposed to have a key?'

'I tell you . . .'

'Save it!' Butteridge snapped. 'Behind that wall you concealed the murdered body of your brother. In here you also concealed the unconscious body of Elva. When you found she had vanished you got the awful feeling that your brother's body had perhaps vanished, too, and that your secret was known to me. You couldn't concoct any reason for looking when I was present, so you came on your own to make sure . . . Just as I knew you would, sooner or later. I was watching for that, Caldon. I followed you all the way from the manor tonight.'

'I didn't come here for anything of the kind!' Drake cried harshly. 'I came to . . .'

'You don't have to talk unless you wish,' Butteridge interrupted. 'Your lawyer can do it for you, but I'm charging you with the murder of Arthur Caldon and Jessie Standish, together with the attempted murder of Elva Caldon. I have to warn you that anything you may say will be taken down in writing and may be used as evidence at your trial.'

Drake clenched his fists. 'You're making a ghastly mistake, inspector. I'm not guilty!'

'I have gathered the facts, Caldon, and it's for the court to do the rest. I'm expressing no opinion — but I may as well tell you that your brother's body is now in Barrington mortuary, and your wife is in protective custody at police headquarters.'

'She's — where?' Drake exclaimed blankly.

'Contrary to what I told you, she was seen last night when she left the manor, and she was followed. You were also seen leaving the manor, and you, too, were followed. You were then kept sight of, but the man who was trailing you heard the screams of your wife behind the door of this cell. He got help from the constable on duty up above. They sent for me, I being the only one with a key to this door. Your wife was rushed to hospital and then discharged. She isn't hurt beyond a severe neck bruise. Evidently a blow that you aimed at the base of her skull, which would have killed her had it landed correctly, missed its mark. Bad light, I suppose. Knowing your homicidal tendencies I kept her in police custody and laid a net for you . . . '

Butteridge shifted position slightly and spread his hands.

'The very fact that you attacked your wife proved your undoing. In her efforts to escape she felt around the wall, found part of it was loose, and pulled it away in an effort to reach the outer world. Her hands contacted a dead body. That was when she screamed for help, and fortunately for her was heard. Naturally, the fact that we found the body and that Arthur supposedly attacked your wife made it obvious that you were the attacker, having changed clothes before leaving the manor, or else somewhere on the way here. As a final point of verification your wife mentioned a cricket ball scar on the shin, which you had shown her. The right shin. I imagine the scar belongs to you.

'I knew just what your reaction would be when you came here and found your wife gone. You would wonder if your twin's body had been found. We built the wall up again, of course, so as to betray nothing to you. I reproach myself for not having looked behind that wall sooner, only I assumed it was sheer age that was causing it to crumble, upon which illusion you, too, doubtless relied. You must have known the police would find the dungeon eventually, but you took the chance that the wall would look innocent. I imagine that your one reason for stopping your wife — or trying to stop her — telling us that perhaps your brother had fixed those car brakes was so that we wouldn't look around the neighbourhood too closely. She acted in spite of you.'

There was silence for a moment. Even Drake's laboured breathing seemed to have ceased. Then Butteridge resumed:

'According to the divisional surgeon's tests your brother has been dead since about the time you were seen with him collecting the rent. Decomposition hasn't progressed fast enough to prevent the cause of death being detected. It was manual strangulation,' Butteridge branched off suddenly into a detailed description of what he believed had happened, and with startling accuracy it matched the hypothesis which Barry Wood had outlined. Drake listened in deadly silence.

'At first,' Butteridge finished, 'every clue pointed to either your brother or Mr. Wood. I never believed any of these false leads, chiefly because of the culprit's slowness in making his escape and also because of the unconvincing method of leaving a pair of brushes all nicely fixed with fingerprints. From the very start I suspected you — even more so when I saw the number of criminological books you possessed. From those you could easily have made an effort to plan a perfect crime and obviate the mistakes of past criminals.

'As to motives — well, maybe you killed Jessie because of her intention to marry your brother. And maybe you killed your brother from sheer dislike. Maybe you tried to kill your wife to stop her finding out too much. Those are the obvious reasons — but according to some of books on psychiatry you might have had another subconscious motive — the desire to rid the world of two imperfect women. I discovered you loved everything just-so when I questioned your wife. For your own sake I'd try to have your lawyer fix a 'guilty but insane' plea.'

Drake straightened up. From grim, silent rage he had moved to cold, towering dignity.

'Insanity is one claim I shall not allow,' he stated calmly. 'I planned everything with cold, calculating logic. I did kill Jessie because she was imperfect. I cannot bear a woman or a man either, or for that matter anything to be imperfect. I killed Arthur because he made a travesty of Nature with his ghastly pictures; I killed

Jessie because of her stump of a finger, which defect I noticed when she served me with petrol. I married Elva and intended to kill her because of her beautiful face and imperfect leg. The very first time I saw her, when I was supposed to be my brother in his car, I made up my mind that she must die. I awaited my best chance; it came when she explored this castle. I had to kill her then because she was trying to identify me with Arthur. Why, when she thought I was asleep she even tried to examine my shin to look for a scar!'

'Keep talking,' Butteridge said briefly.

Drake pushed a hand through his hair. 'I thought I'd mapped it out so perfectly, without a single imperfection. I'm surprised to know the mistakes. I think when perfection crumbles there is nothing for it but to admit the fact, don't you?'

Butteridge shrugged. 'You very nearly did perpetrate a perfect crime, Caldon, if it's any consolation to you. There's one thing only I don't get. What happened last night? Your wife is convinced that she left you in bed, drugged, yet you turned up as your brother and did your best to finish her.'

Drake said: 'She fixed my wine, but stood in front of the mirror over the cocktail cabinet to do it. I saw what happened. I guessed it was intended for me and that she was going to get up to some tricks during the night. I started an argument, during which I switched the tray round so Wood got the drugged wine while I remained clear-headed. I followed my wife here — '

'Did Wood drink too much, or what?' Butteridge interrupted. 'Your wife found him with the wine decanter and — '

'I put them there,' Drake said, brushing the interruption aside. 'Just to prevent her getting suspicious. As I was saying, I followed my wife here, changing on the way. I had a spot where I kept Arthur's clothes, into which I could change in secret at any time. All I had to do was dirty my face and emphasize the beard and moustache line . . . '

Butteridge rubbed his chin pensively. 'While we are on the subject of drugs, I take it that on the night you murdered

Jessica you drugged your wife's wine?'

'Of course,' Drake assented. 'And I arranged the cottage fire with a shielded candle and a petrol trail, first taking away the knife with which I killed Jessie. If you study notes and times I think you'll find I had ample opportunity to do it — also I had the chance to be elsewhere as myself when I was supposed to be my brother.'

'I think,' Butteridge said, 'we had better be on our way. Thanks for the confession. It makes things easier all round.'

'It won't be of any use to you without witnesses,' Drake said slowly. 'Otherwise I wouldn't have made it.'

'No witnesses?' Butteridge raised his voice and shouted. 'Hey, Parker!'

There was a sound in the passage outside and a constable came into the area of the flashlight. Behind him was another man. It was Barry.

'I always have a witness,' Butteridge said, 'though not necessarily in sight — Oh, Mr. Wood!' he exclaimed, surprised.

'I followed my cousin from the manor,' Barry's eyes looked steadily at Drake in the dim light. 'I heard everything, too. I'm pretty amazed at discovering how much I guessed right. I take it, inspector, that I, too, will be arrested?'

'Not by me,' Butteridge answered. 'You haven't done anything.'

'I did my best to kill my cousin in his car.'

'Which he admitted to me and my wife,' Drake said grimly.

'Very well, then.' Butteridge glanced at Drake. 'When we get to headquarters you will have to prefer charges against Mr. Wood.'

A queer smile crossed Drake's face, but he said nothing.

'There is also the matter of my being his business manager in black market deals,' Barry added.

The inspector stared at him. 'Just a minute! You trying to talk yourself into jail, sir?'

'Course not, but I want to make a clean sweep of everything so as to convince Mrs. Caldon that I'm not quite the man she seems to think. I want to explain everything, to prove that I've been a victim of circumstances all along.'

'That,' Butteridge said, 'is inspector Conroy's job, I put him on to both of you, you know.'

For a moment there was silence, then Drake gave an exclamation.

'You! I thought it was Clay who had somehow found our names.'

'No. I found your names through police records and other sources. I had an interview with Clay in prison and found out how much you, Caldon, owed him. He was due to be released and after a talk with Conroy I suggested to Clay that he should call on you and try and collect his money — Clay knowing in advance what sort of a charge Conroy was going to make against you — and thereby verify that you were actually a black marketeer. He did so and told us everything we needed to know. The cheque you gave him to fix things for you was evidence enough in itself.'

'Then — ' Drake's voice broke in fury. 'Then he never had any intention of producing faked books in court?'

'That,' Butteridge responded, 'was

Conroy's idea. Clay enlarged on it and got the £50,000 that was due him. Smart, wasn't he?'

Drake said slowly: 'Got me all sewn up, haven't you? Just like you said? Nice — for a rustic policeman!'

Butteridge motioned outside into the tunnel. Drake began to move towards it, then with a sudden backward movement he lashed out his fist at the inspector's jaw and knocked him flying back against the wall. In the few split seconds that elapsed while he had the advantage Drake snatched his own automatic from the inspector's pocket, turned it on himself and fired. He slumped gradually amidst the rising odour of cordite fumes.

Silence.

'Perhaps,' Butteridge said, pulling himself together and adjusting his umbrella on his arm, 'it's better this way. Deep down he was crazy, you know — quite crazy. He'd got perfection on the brain.'

He bent down and felt for Drake's pulse. There was none. He stood up again and looked at Barry.

'That lets you out, too, Mr. Wood. With

nobody to prefer charges for attempted murder there's nothing we can do. Besides, there are times when even a policeman thinks it's better to forget. As to your being an accessory to Caldon, I don't see how Conroy will be able to prove it. Clay won't, and Caldon can't, and no major deals are in your name.'

'You don't need to say any more, inspector,' Barry said quietly. 'I can see what you're driving at — and thanks.'

'You'd better come back to police headquarters and explain things to Mrs. Caldon. I've the idea she'll be much relieved. Parker, go ahead and telephone for the ambulance to take the body away.'

'Right, sir.'

'Oh, one thing,' Butteridge added, and stooping he drew up Drake's right trouser leg and contemplated a half-healed scar on the shin. 'That's all I wanted to know,' he murmured. 'Let's go.'

CLIMATE INCORPORATED
THE FIVE MATCHBOXES
EXCEPT FOR ONE THING
BLACK MARIA, M.A.
ONE STEP TOO FAR
THE THIRTY-FIRST OF JUNE
THE FROZEN LIMIT
ONE REMAINED SEATED
THE MURDERED SCHOOLGIRL
SECRET OF THE RING
OTHER EYES WATCHING

We do hope that you have enjoyed reading this large print book.

Did you know that all of our titles are available for purchase?

We publish a wide range of high quality large print books including:
Romances, Mysteries, Classics
General Fiction
Non Fiction and Westerns

Special interest titles available in large print are:
The Little Oxford Dictionary
Music Book, Song Book
Hymn Book, Service Book

Also available from us courtesy of Oxford University Press:
Young Readers' Dictionary
(large print edition)
Young Readers' Thesaurus
(large print edition)

For further information or a free brochure, please contact us at:
Ulverscroft Large Print Books Ltd.,
The Green, Bradgate Road, Anstey,
Leicester, LE7 7FU, England.
Tel: (00 44) **0116 236 4325**
Fax: (00 44) **0116 234 0205**

THE RESURRECTED MAN

E. C. Tubb

After abandoning his ship, space pilot Captain Baron dies in space, his body frozen and perfectly preserved. Five years later, doctors Le Maitre and Whitney, restore him to life using an experimental surgical technique. However, returning to Earth, Baron realises that now being legally dead, his only asset is the novelty of being a Resurrected Man. And, being ruthlessly exploited as such, he commits murder — but Inspector McMillan and his team discover that Baron is no longer quite human . . .

THE UNDEAD

John Glasby

On the lonely moor stood five ancient headstones, where a church pointed a spectral finger at the sky. There were those who'd been buried there for three centuries, people who had mingled with inexplicable things of the Dark. People like the de Ruys family, the last of whom had died three hundred years ago leaving the manor house deserted. Until Angela de Ruys came from America, claiming to be a descendant of the old family. Then the horror began . . .